The bear behind me let out a terrifying roar. The sound echoed through the forest.

Then something answered:

AROOOOOOOO!

"Wolves!" I blurted out in disbelief.

No way. Like being chased by a bloodthirsty bear wasn't bad enough?

But there it was again. The bone-chilling howl.

THE HARDY BOYS

Undercover Brothers®

Available from Simon & Schuster

THE HARDY BOYS

Undercover Brothers®

BOYS

FRANKLIN W. DIXON

#35 Lost Brother

BOOK TWO IN THE LOST MYSTERY TRILOGY

WITHDRAWN

Aladdin

New York   London   Toronto   Sydney

This book is a work of fiction. Any references to historical events, real people, or real locales are used fictitiously. Other names, characters, places, and incidents are the product of the author's imagination, and any resemblance to actual events or locales or persons, living or dead, is entirely coincidental.

ALADDIN
An imprint of Simon & Schuster Children's Publishing Division
1230 Avenue of the Americas, New York, NY 10020
First Aladdin paperback edition October 2010
Copyright © 2010 by Simon & Schuster, Inc.
All rights reserved, including the right of reproduction
in whole or in part in any form.
ALADDIN is a trademark of Simon & Schuster, Inc., and related logo is a
registered trademark of Simon & Schuster, Inc.
THE HARDY BOYS MYSTERY STORIES is a trademark
of Simon & Schuster, Inc.
HARDY BOYS UNDERCOVER BROTHERS and related logo are
registered trademarks of Simon & Schuster, Inc.
For information about special discounts for bulk purchases, please
contact Simon & Schuster Special Sales at 1-866-506-1949
or business@simonandschuster.com.
The Simon & Schuster Speakers Bureau can bring authors
to your live event. For more information or to book an event contact
the Simon & Schuster Speakers Bureau at 1-866-248-3049
or visit our website at www.simonspeakers.com.
Designed by Sammy Yuen Jr.
The text of this book was set in Aldine 401 BT.
Manufactured in the United States of America 0910 OFF
10 9 8 7 6 5 4 3 2 1
Library of Congress Control Number 2010924238
ISBN 978-1-4424-0256-0
ISBN 978-1-4424-0257-7 (eBook)

TABLE OF CONTENTS

lind Terror

I was running for my life. It was so dark I could barely see two steps ahead of me. The woods were alive with nighttime sounds—insects buzzing, owls shrieking overhead, the rush of a river somewhere nearby. But the only sound I could focus on was behind me.

The grizzly.

It was huge. When I glanced back, the beast's red-tinged eyes glowed at me out of the darkness.

Close. Way too close.

I pushed myself to run even faster. My lungs and muscles burned.

"Ow!" I shouted as my elbow banged into a tree, sending fireworks of pain through my body.

The bear behind me let out a terrifying roar. The sound echoed through the forest.

Then something answered:

AROOOOOOOO!

"Wolves!" I blurted out in disbelief.

No way. Like being chased by a bloodthirsty bear wasn't bad enough?

But there it was again. The bone-chilling howl.

I ran faster. The wolves kept wailing, sounding closer all the time.

The trail fell away before me. I skidded down a steep hill, trying not to twist an ankle. If I did, I was dead.

At the bottom of the hill, I found myself at the edge of a lake. Its broad, rippled surface gleamed in the moonlight. How far away was the opposite shore? I couldn't tell.

ROAAAAAAR!

The bear was almost on me. What choice did I have? I dove in and started to swim. The water was ice-cold.

By the time I reached the far shore, I was shivering and exhausted. I staggered up onto dry ground, hoping I'd outrun the predators at last.

SPLASH!

I spun around. The bear was just lumbering out of the water! Behind it, I could see the wolf pack swimming fast to catch up. Then an otherworldly cry came from somewhere off to the left. Glancing that way, I saw a mountain lion perched on a ledge, staring down at me.

"No way!" I breathed.

As the big cat leaped down and bounded toward me, I spun around and started running again. My legs felt like waterlogged bags of sand. I knew I wouldn't be able to outrun all those animals for long. But I couldn't give up. An ATAC agent never gives up. . . .

BZZZZZZ!

Uh-oh. Sounded like my cell phone. I was too busy to answer at the moment, but I was pretty sure I knew who was calling. It had to be ATAC HQ. They were probably checking in to see if Joe and I had made any progress on our mission yet.

BZZZZZZ!

"Joe," I murmured, my already thudding heart skipping a beat. Where was my brother?

As I ran, I searched my mind for the answer. Why didn't I know where Joe was? Had the animals gotten him? How had I ended up here, anyway?

Okay. This was weird. Why couldn't I remember where I was or what was happening? It just didn't make sense. . . .

BZZZZZZ!

I sat bolt upright, my heart pounding.

BZZZZZZ!

Whew! It had been a dream! The grizzly, the wolves, the mountain lion, the crazy chase, all of it.

"Oh, man," I murmured, my voice sounding hoarse in the darkness. It was so dark I couldn't see my hand in front of my face.

I reached out, feeling for my alarm clock to hit the off button. My hand hit something hard and unyielding. A wall. A *concrete* wall? Hmm. That was weird.

BZZZZZZ!

I blinked, trying to help my eyes adjust. No dice. I still couldn't see a thing.

That was weird too. My bedroom was never completely dark even at midnight, thanks to the neighbors' porch light. What time was it, anyway?

Lifting my left arm, I was surprised not to see the familiar glow of my ATAC-issue watch. It glows in the dark unless I hit the little button to deactivate that feature. Had I done that before going to sleep?

I felt my left wrist with my other hand. It took a few minutes. For some reason my arms were being a little slow to respond to my brain's commands. I was feeling pretty groggy overall, actually. I figured I must have been deep, deep asleep when I'd been awakened.

BZZZZZZ!

Okay, the buzzing was getting annoying now. Also, I was slowly realizing something else. My alarm clock didn't buzz. It made a sound like a rooster crowing—my aunt Trudy's idea of a fun birthday gift. Joe always said it sounded like a barnyard next door.

That thought helped wake me up a little more. Where *was* I?

I tried to shake the grogginess from my mind. But it wasn't working. I felt as exhausted as if I really had just outrun all those animals from my dream. It didn't help that I also had a raging headache.

BZZZZZZ!

"Focus, Frank," I murmured to myself. Speaking out loud, hearing my own voice, actually made me feel a little more alert. So I kept it up. "My name is Frank Hardy. I live in Bayport, outside New York City. I'm an ATAC agent with my brother Joe. Our latest mission is to investigate a series of disappearances in Misty Falls State Park in Idaho. . . . Oh!"

I blinked in the darkness as the memories began

to ooze back into my brain. I wasn't at home. I was on an ATAC mission. Wasn't I?

BZZZZZZ!

Still feeling fuzzy, I searched my mind for the details.

It had all started in the usual way. ATAC had contacted us about the mission. Dad had helped run interference with Mom and Aunt Trudy, who didn't know about ATAC. Dad knows, of course, since he started the group. ATAC—American Teens Against Crime—sends teenage agents out to investigate cases where adults might raise suspicion. In this case, we were posing as students writing a paper on a series of missing kids known as the Misty Falls Lost.

Joe and I had flown out to Misty Falls, Idaho, and met Detective Richard Cole, who had filled us in on all the details. Over the past twelve years, eight children had disappeared while camping at the ruggedly beautiful state park. One of the kids' remains had turned up later in a bear cave, though none of the others had ever been found. Still, most people had seemed willing to believe they'd all fallen prey to wild animals or other natural causes.

Until one of the kids returned.

"Justin Greer," I murmured, the name swimming out of the fog in my mind.

Joe and I had been called in when Justin, one of the Misty Falls Lost, had turned up with no memory of who he was or where he'd been for the past dozen years. His reappearance had reopened the case, and things had only gotten weirder from there.

But nothing quite as weird as this. Where *was* I?

I squeezed my eyes shut, trying to focus. The last thing I could remember was being at our campsite in the park. A big grizzly had turned up and taken a swipe at Joe.

That explained my weird dream, I guess. But why couldn't I remember what had happened next? Had the bear gotten me, too? Was I in the hospital? And what had happened to Joe? Was he okay?

Panic grabbed at me again. I didn't know the answers to any of those questions, and I didn't like that feeling. I like knowing what's going on, having all the facts in order. It's kind of my thing.

I realized the buzzing noise had finally stopped. That was a relief.

Shoving back the scratchy blanket, I carefully swung my feet around, searching for the edge of the bed I was on. When I felt cool metal beneath my hands, I realized it was more like a cot.

My feet touched a hard, cool, smooth floor. I

pushed off with my arms, staggering to my feet. It was still too dark to see anything, so I felt my way around.

Smooth concrete walls forming a room about six feet square. The cot. The outline of a door, tightly closed with no handle and only a tiny slit of a window at around eye level.

Nothing else. No light switch, nada.

I stood there in the darkness, swaying slightly and trying to think through the fuzz still coating my mind. My ATAC training had prepared me for a lot. But not for anything like this.

Feeling my way back over to the door, I peered through the little window. Or tried to, anyway. I couldn't see a thing.

That pushed my panic up another notch.

"Help!" I shouted, pounding on the door. "Somebody! Where am I? Help! *Let me out of here!*"

ead Ends

It takes a lot to make me panic. But I was panicking now. Big-time. "Dude, there's *got* to be a clue out here somewhere!" I said for about the millionth time.

Detective Rich Cole shot me a sympathetic look. "Don't worry, Joe," he said, pushing back the brim of his cowboy hat. "We're not going to give up until we find Frank."

I nodded and crashed forward through a thicket of brambles. Ouch. Thorns dug into my bare arms, drawing blood. But I ignored the pain. Nothing mattered except finding my brother.

Detective Cole and I had been searching the woods around the campsite for at least an hour.

Maybe more. It's hard to keep track of time when you're freaking out.

There was one solution to that, of course.

I needed to stop freaking out.

Stopping for a second, I took a few deep breaths. Looked up through the trees at the clear blue morning sky. Tried to focus on my ATAC training. I had to get myself under control, or there wasn't much chance I'd be able to help my brother.

"Okay." I turned toward Rich, who was right behind me. "Let's go over what happened one more time. Figure out if we're missing something important."

Rich looked a little surprised by my new calm, cool, collected attitude. But he nodded.

"We know Officer Donnelly wouldn't have left Frank alone without good reason," he said. "Someone must have lured him away, then knocked him out with a blow to the head."

Donnelly was another cop. He'd been helping Rich guard Frank and me at our camp the night before.

Why do a couple of highly trained, super-awesome ATAC agents need police protection? Good question. It was because we'd been pretty sure someone was after us. For each of our first three nights at camp, we'd found letters scratched into the dirt. The first night, just an *L*. The second night, it was *LO*. Then *LOS*. Detective Cole had decided we might need some help before it turned into *LOST*—as in, another addition to the Misty Falls Lost. So he and Officer Donnelly had camped out with us to make sure we didn't run into any trouble.

Unfortunately, trouble ran right into us anyway. A big grizzly had crashed the party and taken a swipe at me. It was only a flesh wound, but Rich had insisted on taking me to the hospital anyway. When we got back, Officer Donnelly was out cold and Frank was gone.

Lost.

"We'll have to see if Officer Donnelly remembers anything when he wakes up," I said. "But we can't wait around until then."

Rich had called the hospital a few minutes earlier for an update. Donnelly was going to be fine, but he'd be sleeping off the drugs for a few more hours.

"Right," Rich agreed. "It's pretty clear we're not dealing with an animal attack this time."

"Check this out, guys!" a new voice said.

I turned. It was a park ranger, an outdoorsy brunette in her thirties named Bailey Cooper. Rich had called her in to help us search the area. Well, her and every available cop in a hundred-mile radius. Which in rural Idaho, translated to maybe a dozen people.

We hurried toward Bailey. She was peering at some shrubs.

"Look." She pointed to a branch.

It looked pretty much like every other branch around there. Wild. Prickly.

"Um, what are we looking at?" I asked.

She shot me a look. "Oh, right," she said. "City slicker."

Rich chuckled. I rolled my eyes. Yeah, it was pretty obvious she was joking, but the joke was getting a little old. Everyone in Misty Falls seemed to think Frank and I were hopeless just because we hadn't been raised like mountain men.

Bailey was a pretty sharp cookie. She seemed to guess what I was thinking and moved on.

"Looks like someone's been this way fairly recently," she said in a brisk, professional voice. "See? These little end branches are all bent over or broken, and the breaks are still green and fresh. And they're high up—around shoulder height. Might've just been a deer or bear passing through, or . . ."

"Lead the way," Rich told her. "It's worth checking out."

The two of us followed Bailey down the trail. If you could call it that. It was pretty wild. But Bailey kept pointing out more broken branches and stuff, so we kept at it.

I didn't mind the rough going. It distracted me from worrying about Frank. A little, anyway.

Then I spotted something out of the corner of my eye. It was a little pile of rocks. Not the natural kind either. It was obvious that these rocks had been stacked on purpose.

"What's that?" I said, pointing.

Bailey came back to look. "Hmm, haven't seen these in this part of the park," she said. "There are lots of them out in the wilder areas, though."

"What are they?"

"Not sure." She shrugged. "Some kind of primitive trail marker, maybe. Like the Inukshuk that the Inuit and other native peoples make. We're not far north enough to be in Inuit country, of course, but I suppose the native tribes in this area might have developed similar types of markers."

I stared at the little stack of stones. I'd heard of Inukshuk and stuff like that. But the little pile of stones made me think of something else. Namely, *The Blair Witch Project*. Like a lot of things about this park, the stone marker seemed to come straight out of that creepy film.

"Then again, this could just be the work of a young visitor messing around playing wilderness guide or something," Bailey went on. Then she frowned. "Not that there have been many little kids camping around here lately . . ."

Yeah, no kidding. Eight unexplained disappearances in twelve years can really put a damper on the family-friendly appeal of a place. Even if you believed it was all the work of hungry bears. Maybe *especially* if you believed it was the work of hungry bears.

Not that I believed that. Not at all. Sure, there were bears around. The gash on my shoulder was proof of that.

But no bear had scratched LOST in the dirt in front of our tent. Or injected Officer Donnelly with drugs. Or broken into Farley O'Keefe's cabin and stabbed him to death . . .

Farley. In all the panic of the past few hours, I'd all but forgotten about him. He'd been the head ranger at the park for years. He was a crusty old coot who seemed way more comfortable out in the wilderness than he could ever be in civilization.

"If this is a trail marker of some kind, I wonder if Farley had something to do with it?" I mused as I snapped a few photos of the weird little stone pile with my ATAC-issue cell phone. "Seems like his type of thing."

"Won't argue with you there," Rich agreed. "Ol' Farley knew all the backcountry tricks. Wish he was still around to ask about this."

He shook his head sadly. I stared at the pile of stones. Frank and I had wondered if Farley might have been involved in the case. Especially after learning that he was Justin Greer's biological grandfather—a fact that even Rich hadn't known. Were we too hasty to cross Farley off the suspect list just because he was dead? What if he'd had an accomplice—someone who'd killed him, then taken Frank?

Okay, maybe it was a little far-fetched as theories go. But it was pretty much all I had. . . .

SUSPECT PROFILE

Name: Farley O'Keefe

Hometown: Misty Falls, Idaho

Physical description: Currently deceased; when alive, 6'0", 185 pounds, 75 years old, silver-gray hair and close-cropped beard, dark brown eyes, hooked nose

<u>Occupation</u>: Was head ranger at Misty Falls State Park.

<u>Background</u>: Lost a son in Desert Storm, lost his wife eighteen months ago, recently discovered to be the biological grandfather of Justin Greer.

<u>Suspicious behavior</u>: Seemed determined to convince everyone that the disappearances in the park were due to animals and other natural causes. Kept his relationship with Justin secret even after his return.

<u>Suspected of</u>: Being involved in the case, along with accomplice(s) unknown.

<u>Possible Motive</u>: Wanting Justin to stay with him instead of his adoptive parents.

"So I guess Farley spent a lot of time out in the woods alone, huh?" I asked Bailey as we moved on, still following the faint trail of broken branches.

She glanced at me and shrugged. "Got me," she said. "I didn't know him all that well. I only transferred up here a few months ago. Till then

I worked at a different park downstate."

"Oh." Another dead end. That pretty much described this mission so far.

The trail we were following quickly petered out too. We circled back to the campsite. A police photographer was getting some shots of the LOST scrawled in the dirt. Another cop was sifting through the stuff from our tent.

I was feeling restless and on the verge of panicking again. To distract myself, I scouted around the clearing where we'd been camping, hoping to hit on some clue we'd missed earlier.

No luck. But on my way back from the river, I noticed a broken branch at the edge of the woods. It was shoulder high—just like the ones on the trail Bailey had been following earlier.

I pushed past it, looking for another trail. Maybe some sign that Frank and/or his attacker had come this way.

Instead I found myself stepping into a small open area. It was behind some bushy undergrowth, all but hidden from the main clearing.

And right in the middle was another weird little little pile of rocks!

My heart pounded as I crouched down beside it for a better look. The stone pile wasn't identical to the other one, but it was close. How long had it been there? Could there be fingerprints on the stones—maybe left by Frank's abductor?

"Wish I had JuDGE with me," I muttered.

That was our favorite gadget—more properly known as Junior Data Gathering Equipment. It was wirelessly connected to ATAC's mainframe computer and could get any evidence analyzed within hours. Just because I happened to break the thing a time or six, Frank refuses to let me carry it anymore. It had almost certainly been in his pocket as usual when he'd disappeared.

Anyway, it didn't matter. The police or the rangers should be able to help me out.

"Yo, Rich!" I shouted, still crouched down beside the little pile of stones. "Come check this out!"

I waited for an answering shout, but instead heard a very different sound. An ominous rattle.

Spinning around, I gasped. A huge rattlesnake was coiled to strike right behind me! My eyes widened and my muscles tensed. But it was too late to get away.

Before I could move, the snake struck, its deadly fangs shooting toward my bare arm.

act-Checking

Have you ever spent any time in complete and utter darkness? Let me tell you, it's not fun. It plays weird tricks on your mind. Like making every passing minute feel like an hour. Or sometimes like two seconds.

I'd spent a few of those seconds-minutes-hours pounding on the door. Then I'd woken up a little more and realized that was a waste of energy. After getting myself back under control, I'd sat down on the edge of the cot to try to figure out what to do.

That had been about half an hour ago. Maybe. Like I said, it was hard to keep track of the time. But however long it had been, I was no closer to any answers.

"Let's be logical about this," I murmured under my breath. "This has to have something to do with our mission."

I thought about that, turning it over in my mind. Doing my "Mr. Logic" thing, as Joe would say.

So sue me. I like to think before I act.

Besides, being logical made me feel a little better. A little more in control. So I kept at it, staring into the darkness while I thought about everything that had happened. The parts I could remember, anyway.

No matter which way I looked at things, I kept reaching the same conclusion. I'd been taken by the same person or people who'd taken Justin and all those other kids. Nothing else made sense.

When I thought about it that way, the situation had a silver lining. Sure, I was stuck in a dark cell somewhere with no idea how I got here. And even less about how I was going to get out.

But Joe and I hadn't been making much progress on our mission up until now. Maybe this was just the break we needed. Maybe now I'd be able to figure things out from the inside.

"Okay," I muttered. "So now what?"

The longer I sat there, the clearer my mind felt. But it was still working more slowly than usual.

Plus, I still couldn't remember anything beyond that bear attack, and I was pretty sure I knew why.

I'd been drugged. It was the only explanation for the weird grogginess. Not to mention the vivid, crazy dreams.

To clear my head, I decided to go over the facts of the case again. Who were our suspects?

"Well, Farley is out," I murmured, flashing back to the gruesome scene in the ranger's cabin the evening before. No way he'd been the one who'd brought me here.

But there was at least one other suspect still at large. Jacob Greer, Justin's adoptive father. The guy seemed pretty conflicted about having his son back. Was he just upset because Justin didn't remember him, or much of anything else about his old life? Or was there some darker reason? Either way, Jacob clearly had a temper.

"Wait," I whispered into the darkness, straining to remember. "Didn't Jacob go back home to Chicago?"

I was pretty sure he had. But I still didn't completely trust my mind. What if whatever had happened to bring me here wasn't the only hole in my memory? What if I was still missing big chunks of the past and didn't even realize it?

The thought made me even more panicky than not knowing where I was. To test myself, I decided to run through the list of the Misty Falls Lost.

"Justin was the first victim; he disappeared

almost twelve years ago," I recited. "Next came Kerry, an eight-year-old girl who went missing from her campsite a year later. Then Sarah, age five, two years after that. Next came Luke, a seven-year-old boy who disappeared while sleeping in his family's car. Alice, age four, the only child to go missing during daylight hours, while on a walk with her older brother. Next was Tommy, age eight. Or was it Kyle? No," I corrected myself, feeling more confident with each name I remembered. "It was Tommy, *then* Kyle. And then Ellie, a six-year-old who disappeared just last year."

There. I was pretty sure I had the whole list right. Whew! Maybe my brain wasn't turning into swiss cheese after all. Now if I could only remember how I'd ended up here . . . wherever "here" was . . .

Okay, I admit it. Even at my most logical, it was tough to sit there pondering the mission in a totally dark room. It was starting to mess with my head.

I stood up and felt my way around the dark little space again, hoping I'd missed something.

Nope. All that was in there was me and the cot.

I stopped at the door, feeling carefully around it. There was no handle on this side, as I'd already noted. No hinges, either.

My fingers explored the tiny, narrow window. The glass felt pretty thick. I banged at it with the heel of one hand, but my hand definitely took the worst of it. The glass didn't budge.

There wasn't anything in the room I could use to try to break it. Now that I thought about it, I realized I wasn't even wearing shoes.

That seemed kind of weird. Had I been sleeping when I was taken?

I felt my clothes. Loose-fitting V-neck shirt. Drawstring pants. As best I could tell, I seemed to be wearing something like hospital scrubs.

I don't own hospital scrubs.

"Weird," I murmured.

The pants had pockets, but there was nothing in them. No surprise there. If my watch was gone, there wasn't much chance my cell phone would still be on me. Or JuDGE. Or my flashlight. Or any of the other stuff I'd kept on me night and day during this mission.

I pressed my face against the window, trying to see anything on the other side. But all that met my gaze was more blackness. Either it was equally dark on the other side, or there was something covering the glass. I couldn't tell which.

Turning away, I stared into the darkness, trying to make sense of all this. But the only thing I knew for sure was that those kids hadn't just fallen prey to bears or the river or whatever.

"Or to ghosts, either," I whispered with a grimace.

That was Joe's nuttiest theory. He'd paid a little too much attention to some local ghost stories.

I'd never believed that, of course. Mr. Logic, remember? But if there'd been doubt, it was gone.

A ghost hadn't drugged me. A bear hadn't locked me in this dark, featureless room. No, someone—a person, or people—had taken me, just as he/she/they had taken all those kids over the years.

But why? We obviously weren't dealing with your run-of-the-mill serial killer. Otherwise Justin couldn't have come back. I wouldn't still be alive.

CLANG!

Suddenly a blinding light shot into the room. I stumbled back, half-blinded after all that time in utter darkness.

I was so startled that it took me a second to realize what had happened. Someone had flipped open whatever was covering the little window in the door, allowing light from outside to come in.

"Hey!" I shouted, leaping toward the door. "Who's out there?"

I squinted, desperately trying to force my eyes to adjust so I could look out.

CLANG!

Too late. The window shut again, returning me to total darkness.

urprising Outbursts

*B*ANG!

"AAAAH!" I yelled, falling back as the snake suddenly exploded in front of me. *Right* in front of me. I actually felt the creature's fangs scrape across my skin as it flew into the air.

Panting with adrenaline, I glanced back and saw Detective Cole standing there, his service revolver still pointed toward me. Or rather, toward the rattler.

"You okay, Joe?" Rich quickly holstered the gun and hurried toward me.

"Yeah." I jumped to my feet, casting a wary glance at the snake. Or what was left of it. "Nice shot. Oh, and thanks."

"No problem." The detective bent over me,

examining my arm. "Looks like I wasn't a second too soon—it was about to take a chunk out of you."

"What was that? Who's shooting in here?" Bailey pushed her way into the little clearing. When she saw the dead rattler, she blanched. "Oh no! Why'd you do that?"

Rich shot her a look. "Why do you think?"

"And why do you care?" I added, shuddering as I glanced at the rattler again. "It's not like rattle-snakes are an endangered species or anything, right?"

She frowned. "That's not the point. I hate to see any wild creature harmed by humans. Even rattle-snakes have their place in the ecosystem. In fact, we keep an injured one in captivity at the ranger station so people can see it up close—through a layer of protective glass, of course—and face their fears in a rational way. Maybe even come to appreciate the beauty of the species."

Rich raised an eyebrow. "Oh? I thought that captive rattler was there to show folks what they look like. You know—so they can avoid them out here."

Bailey shrugged. "That's another reason, I suppose. But a lot of people are way too quick to demonize wild animals for anything and everything. In fact, that's the whole reason I asked for a transfer to this park."

"Huh?" I said. "What do you mean?"

She suddenly looked like she wished she hadn't said anything. "Just what I said," she replied slowly. "You know. Because of all the lost kids. People were blaming bears, acting like they were all killers. That's a dangerous way to think. Dangerous for the bears, and for all wildlife and wild places like this park."

Interesting. I glanced at Rich. He rolled his eyes so Bailey couldn't see. I guessed he thought she was kind of a kook.

And maybe she was. But I couldn't help recalling that Farley had been one of those people who'd loudly and frequently insisted that those kids had disappeared due to bears or other natural causes. And now he was dead. Could there be a connection?

"So if it wasn't bears, what do you think happened to all those kids?" I asked Bailey, trying to keep my voice casual.

She shook her head. "Wish I knew. I've been poking around, trying to figure it out."

Meanwhile Rich was staring at my arm again. "We'd better get you to the hospital, Joe," he said. "It doesn't look like the snake broke the skin, but better safe than sorry."

I groaned. "Again?" I complained, glancing down at the bandage poking out from beneath my shirt.

Courtesy of that bear attack a few hours earlier. "They're going to have to name a wing after me soon!"

Rich grinned. "Come on," he said. "I'll drive you."

A couple of hours later I was still at Mercy Hospital. Not because of the snakebite—the docs had cleared me on that. But I'd figured as long as I was there, I might as well stop by and check in with Justin. See if he'd remembered else anything yet. Especially anything that might help me find Frank.

I knew the cops were still searching the park. But I was starting to think that was a waste of time. After all, nobody had ever found anything useful when those kids had disappeared. Why should we expect anything different now? No, if I wanted to find my brother, I was going to have to figure out another way.

It was late morning, and I had the waiting room to myself. I checked my watch, then went and peered down the hall toward Justin's door. Still closed.

"Hurry up, dude!" I muttered under my breath, feeling impatient.

When I'd tried to go in, the nurses had stopped me. They'd said Dr. Carrini was in there having a private session with Justin.

Carrini was some big-shot memory expert from the nearest university hospital. He'd been spending a lot of time in Misty Falls trying to help Justin get his memory back.

He definitely wasn't the warm and fuzzy type of doctor, though. When he gave an order, he expected to be obeyed. I knew better than to interrupt him now.

But it was tempting. The longer I sat in that waiting room—or, rather, paced restlessly back and forth—the more impatient I felt. As if time was literally ticking away for Frank.

And the longer I waited, the more the truth sank in. If I wanted to find my brother, I needed to figure out this case. But Frank wasn't going to be there to help me this time.

It was a weird thought. Very weird.

"Man, could I use some of his nerdy theories right about now," I murmured.

See, that's the thing about Frank. He might be kind of a nerd, especially compared to me. But he's also supersmart. Sure, I have plenty of great ideas. But he's the one who turns them into workable plans.

See what I mean? We were a well-oiled team. That's why we'd been able to solve so many tough missions. *Together.*

But now I was on my own. I just had to deal with that and do my best. Frank's life could depend on it.

"But no pressure," I whispered with a shiver.

I quickly shoved away that thought. If I was going to do this without Frank, maybe it was time to try thinking like him. So what would my brainiac brother do if he were here now?

"What do you think, dude?" I said aloud, trying to picture Frank standing there in the waiting room with me. "What's our next step?

"Well, my incredibly studly and awesome brother," I said in a slightly nerdier tone, doing my best to channel Frank's response, "we should look at things logically. You know, indubitably and stuff."

My shoulders slumped slightly. Okay, my Frank impression was pretty spot-on. But I was going to need more than that. . . .

"We aren't finding much in the way of clues," I pointed out to imaginary Frank. "And our suspects keep dying."

I could almost see imaginary Frank roll his eyes. He hates when I exaggerate.

"Only one suspect has died so far, my incredibly illogical yet astoundingly handsome brother," I said in my stuffy imaginary-Frank voice. I started pacing again as I thought hard about what Frank might say next. "In any case, we shall have to explore other avenues of cluedom. Perhaps your brilliant idea of talking with Justin again shall produce some breakthrough."

I sighed, stopping again just long enough to peer down the hall. Then I turned and wandered back across the waiting room, almost imagining I really could see Frank standing there looking dorky and thoughtful.

"Doubtful, bro," I told imaginary Frank. "This Carrini dude might be some big expert and all. But so far he hasn't managed to get Justin to remember much. At least not anything important."

Imaginary Frank nodded wisely, looking smug. I usually hated when he looked like that. But this time I was eager to hear what he—er, I—would say next.

"Then perhaps it's time to try something new," I blurted out in my imaginary-Frank voice. "Dr. Carrini is being cautious, and that's fine for his purposes. But we need a breakthrough. What if we took Justin back to the spot in town where he first reappeared last week? That might jar his memory enough so he—"

"Joe! Who are you talking to in here?"

I spun around, feeling my face go beet red. A pretty girl with dark, curly hair was standing there staring at me.

"Chloe!" I blurted out. "Uh, I didn't hear you come in."

Yeah. That much was obvious.

Chloe looked a little confused. She was a friendly candy striper we'd met on our first visit to the hospital. *Really* friendly. Especially toward Frank. For some reason, girls always go for him. It's really annoying.

"Listen," I said. "I know it probably looks like I was standing here talking to myself, but—"

"It's okay, Joe." Her face went all gooey and sympathetic. "I heard what happened at the park this morning. You must be super freaked out and worried. I came to let you know Dr. Carrini just finished. If you want to see Justin, come on in. But I should warn you, he's pretty tired."

"I know how he feels."

That was the truth. I hadn't had a good night's sleep since arriving in Idaho.

She shot me that sympathetic smile again. "I hope you'll let me know when you find Frank," she said. "I have the day off from the hospital tomorrow, but please call me on my cell if he turns up, okay? If I don't answer, just leave a message."

Before I could respond, my own cell phone buzzed in my pocket. I grabbed it, with a flash of crazy hope that it was Frank calling. That somehow this was all some big misunderstanding and he'd just gotten lost on his way to the latrine or something.

But no. The caller ID screen read BAILEY COOPER.

"Hurry," Chloe said, already hurrying off down the hall. "Justin looked ready to fall asleep when Dr. C. left."

I tucked the phone back into my pocket. If Bailey had found anything important, she would have called Rich first. Whatever she wanted to talk to me about could wait.

Jogging a few steps, I caught up with Chloe. Dr. Carrini was leaning on the counter at the nurses' station, writing notes on a chart. I nodded politely and scooted into Justin's room.

Justin was lying in his bed looking pale and kind of sleepy. Nobody who didn't know better would guess what had happened to him. He looked like an ordinary kid in his late teens. Maybe in the hospital to repair a high school football injury. Or to have his appendix out. Something normal like that.

But I knew better. His case was anything but normal. And if you knew where to look, you could see it. The hint of wildness in his eyes.

Yeah. Definitely not normal.

"Hi, Joe," he said with a yawn as Chloe straightened his blanket. "What are you doing here?"

"I need to talk to you, Justin," I said. "Did anyone tell you the news?"

He yawned again, deeper this time. "What news?" His voice was already sounding fainter.

"About my brother Frank. He went missing this morning. Like, early this morning, probably when it was still dark out. . . ."

"Aaaaaaaaaah!" Justin suddenly sat bolt upright, letting out an unearthly shriek. His eyes had gone wide and were staring right past me. "The darkness! The darkness!"

"What?" I traded a glance with Chloe, who looked as startled and confused as I felt.

Out in the hall, I already heard voices and running feet. A second later Dr. Carrini burst in, along with a nurse or two.

"I remember! I remember!" Justin babbled, tears rolling down his cheeks and his hands clenched on the bedclothes. "The dark place. Oh, it was horrible!"

"Back away, please," Carrini said sternly to Chloe and me. He hurried forward, producing a syringe from his pocket. With a practiced move, he uncapped it and plunged it into Justin's upper arm.

A second later Justin slumped forward, his eyes drooping shut. He let out a sigh, relaxing his death grip on the sheet.

Carrini turned to glare at me. "What did you say to him?" he demanded. "I won't have outsiders upsetting my patient! Who gave you permission to come in here, anyway?"

"Look," I blurted out, too on edge myself to be polite. "I didn't mean to upset anyone, but I'm pretty upset right now myself, okay? In case you didn't hear, my brother disappeared from the park this morning, and I really need to figure out what happened to him!"

Carrini looked surprised. "He did?" he said. "I'm sorry to hear that. I hope you find him soon."

Okay, that made me feel pretty stupid for losing it like that. "Thanks," I murmured, slinking out of the room.

Stopping in the hall outside, I wondered what to do next. I pulled out my phone, but Bailey hadn't left a message. Guess it hadn't been anything important after all.

I yawned. My busy morning and lack of sleep was catching up with me. There was only one solution to that. I needed some serious caffeine. And something to eat. It was almost lunchtime by now.

I headed to the hospital cafeteria. It was nearly as deserted as the waiting room had been. I grabbed a banana, then headed for the coffee station out near the tables.

"Fancy meeting you here," Rich said from behind me just as I reached for the coffeepot. "Looks like you needed some coffee too."

"For sure." I poured my own cup, then filled the one he held up. "Have a second to talk?"

"Sure."

We sat down and started to discuss the case. Not that there was much to discuss. Rich had just checked in on Officer Donnelly, who was still unconscious and probably would be for a while yet. I mentioned Bailey's call, but Rich hadn't heard from her. He also hadn't heard from the cops searching the park, which meant they probably hadn't found anything yet.

"No surprise there," I said ruefully, taking a sip of my coffee. "Whoever did this seems to be pretty good at—"

I cut myself off as a college-age kid rushed into the cafeteria. I'd never seen him before, and probably wouldn't have paid any attention to him now.

Except for one thing. He was brandishing a huge butcher knife!

Racing up to one of the cafeteria workers, he waved the knife at her in a threatening way.

"I heard Justin Greer is in the hospital!" the kid shouted. "I demand to talk to Justin Greer! *Right now!*"

eing the Light

I jumped as an overhead light clicked on. The glare was blinding at first, forcing me to squeeze my eyes shut as I staggered to my feet. But finally I was able to crack them open and take my first real look around.

I wasn't sure how much time had passed since the window in the door had opened and closed. Like I said, it was hard to keep track. Especially since I was pretty sure I'd zoned out for a while.

Blinking rapidly to help my eyes finish adjusting, I stared at my surroundings. I wasn't sure how long this light would last.

Bare cement walls, check. Small cot, check. Metal door with no handle or hinges showing, check.

Glancing up, I saw the overhead light glaring down from a ceiling at least fifteen feet over my head. The bulb was encased in a metal cage. Beside it was a grate that looked like some kind of speaker.

As my eyes slid down the wall again, they stopped on something. I blinked, still having trouble focusing after so long in total darkness. Leaning on the bed, I peered at the whitewashed wall near the pillow.

Someone had scratched something into the wall's hard surface. It looked like the notch marks someone might make to keep track of passing days—like the ones in prison cells all over the world.

Someone had been marking time in here before me. If I was here much longer, I might have to try that myself.

I was about to turn away when I saw more markings beneath the first ones. These were even fainter, partially obscured by the rumpled blanket and pillow. I had to actually kneel on the cot and push the bedding aside to get a good look.

When I did, I let out a gasp. The first line was a single word: LOST. And below that, fainter still, a name: LUKE.

My mind immediately flashed to the list of Misty Falls Lost victims. One of them was a boy named Luke!

"Whoa," I whispered, trying to wrap my head around what this meant. Could that same Luke have been held here in this room, just as I was being held now?

Almost involuntarily, my eyes darted around the tiny room. As if I was expecting to see a little boy peering out at me from some shadowy corner.

Then I got ahold of myself again. Okay, this whole case was pretty creepy. But I wasn't going to give in to that. I had to stay focused.

CLANG!

I spun around, almost falling off the cot. The door had just swung partly open!

"Hey!" I yelled, lunging forward.

ZZZZZP.

I had to stop short to avoid tripping over something that had just slid in through the partially open door. A tray. I couldn't see who'd slid it in, since the door opened toward me, blocking any view of whatever was outside.

CLANG!

The door swung shut again. I leaped forward and grabbed at it, my knuckles scraping painfully on the metal. But it was no good. I collapsed against the door as I heard a bolt slide shut on the other side.

"Please!" I called. "Who's there? Why are you keeping me here?"

No answer. I just leaned there for a second, feeling hopeless. Then I turned to look down at the tray.

There was food on it. A sandwich on a paper plate. An apple. A plastic cup of water. A thin paper napkin.

My stomach let out a sudden grumble. I realized I was ravenous. How long had it been since I'd eaten? I had no idea, but my digestive system was telling me it had been way too long.

I picked up the tray and stared at the food. It smelled delicious. The sandwich was tuna salad—one of my favorites. My fingers twitched, ready to pick up the sandwich and cram it into my mouth.

"No," I whispered, setting the tray down again.

I was famished. And still a little groggy. But I hadn't completely lost my mind—or my ATAC training. And that training warned me to be suspicious. What if this meal was drugged?

I could survive being hungry for a while longer. If I passed out again due to some weird tranquilizer, I might never get out of here.

Sitting down on the edge of the cot, I stared at the door. The scent of tuna drifted through the air, making my stomach grumble constantly, but I did my best to ignore it.

If someone opened that door again, I wanted to be ready.

More time passed. How much? You got me.

I was trying to stay alert. But it wasn't easy. I caught myself dozing off a few times. Each time it was harder to pull myself out of it.

CLANG!

I jerked awake, realizing I'd done it again. Springing forward, I crashed into the door, scrabbling for the edge, planning to yank it open and face whoever was out there.

Oops. The door was still shut tight.

Then I realized where the clanging noise had come from this time. The little window. It was open again! A set of eyes was peering in.

"Hello?" I called. "Who's there?"

The eyes pulled back. I pressed my face to the window and looked out.

A little girl who looked about ten years old was standing in a featureless hallway outside. She stared at me with wide blue eyes. Her long, auburn hair was braided into pigtails.

"Who are you?" she asked, her high-pitched voice muffled by the thick metal door. "Are you staying here now?"

"I'm Frank," I called back. "Who are you?"

She didn't answer for a second as she looked

up and down the hall. Then her big blue eyes returned to me.

"Do you know where my brother is?" she asked, sounding plaintive now. "They won't tell me. Have you seen him?"

"Where are we?" I asked. "What is this place?"

"I really want to find my brother," the little girl said with a sigh. "Are you sure you don't know where he is? I thought you might know."

"Um, I'm not sure," I said, just wanting to keep her talking. "What's your name?"

"I'm Alice."

I gasped. That was another name from the victims' list! Alice was the name of a little girl who'd disappeared five or six years ago while she was on a nature walk with her teenage brother. The brother had been unconscious when they'd found him, with no idea where his sister had gone.

Unless I missed my guess, I was talking to another of the Misty Falls Lost!

ew Suspicions

Rich was a pro. I'm no slouch either, thanks to my ATAC training. It took the two of us only seconds to grab the college-age kid and wrestle the knife out of his hand.

"Hey!" he yelped as Rich whipped his hands around behind his back. "Let me go!"

"Sorry, son," Rich said in his best sheriff's drawl. "Afraid I can't do that. Not until you tell me exactly what you were hoping to accomplish by waving that blade around at innocent people."

The kid sort of slumped against his restraint, probably realizing it was pointless to struggle. He was average height and weight with reddish brown hair. He didn't stand a chance against Rich, who probably outweighed him by almost a hundred pounds.

"I need to talk to Justin Greer," he said, sounding kind of sullen. "I just heard he was here, and I really, really need to talk to him."

"Mind telling me why?" said Rich.

The kid stared at him. Then he glanced around at the cafeteria workers and other onlookers.

"It's private," he said after a second. "But it's, like, really important, okay?"

"If it's that important, you'd better spill it," I said. "Maybe we can help. Are you a friend of Justin's or something?"

The kid turned to stare at me. "Who are you?"

"Don't bother, Joe," Rich growled. "He's probably just another true-crime junkie. We've had a few of 'em show up here over the years."

"Hang on," I said as Rich started to wrestle the kid toward the door. The detective rolled his eyes impatiently but stopped. I smiled at the kid. "My name's Joe," I told him. "What's yours?"

For a second I didn't think he was going to answer. Finally he spit out, "Stanley."

"Cool. So, Stanley, where are you from?" I asked.

This time the pause was even longer. "Seattle," he said at last.

"What brings you out here to see Justin?" I asked, trying to sound friendly. "Did you know him before he disappeared?"

Stanley seemed to have run out of answers. At least ones he was willing to share. No matter what Rich and I said after that, he refused to give us any more information.

"You might as well lock me up or whatever," he told Rich at last with a frown.

Rich shrugged. "Your wish is my command. Few hours cooling off in the pokey might jog your memory." He glanced at me. "You want a ride into town?"

"No thanks, I'm okay," I said.

I watched him drag Stanley off. Weird. Was the kid really a true-crime fan, like the cop thought? Or could something else be going on here?

"But what?" I whispered to myself. Stanley was several years older than Justin, so it seemed unlikely they'd been best buddies before the disappearance. So what was this kid after? Should he be on my suspect list?

I pulled out my phone, tempted to shoot off an e-mail to ask HQ to look into it. But what would I say? I hadn't thought to snap a photo of the guy, and I didn't even know his last name. . . .

SUSPECT PROFILE

<u>Name:</u> Stanley (last name unknown)

<u>Hometown:</u> Seattle, Washington

<u>Physical description:</u> 5'10", 160 pounds, approximately 20 years old, reddish brown hair, blue eyes, dressed in jeans and T-shirt

<u>Occupation:</u> Unknown—possible college student (??)

<u>Suspicious behavior:</u> Burst into Mercy Hospital waving a knife and demanding to see Justin Greer.

<u>Suspected of:</u> Unknown

<u>Possible motive:</u> Unknown

I sighed, deciding I needed a little more to go on before getting ATAC involved with this one. Even HQ couldn't do much with what I had so far.

While I had my phone out, I clicked through the missed-call list to get Bailey's number, then tried to call her back. No answer—it went straight to voice mail. I left a quick message, then hung up.

I walked back to my cooling coffee and chugged it, trying to decide what to do next. Should I head into town, follow up on this Stanley thing? It seemed too weird to dismiss completely. But I wasn't sure how it could possibly relate to Frank's disappearance. And I didn't want to get caught up with some red herring while my brother's trail went cold.

Figuring Stanley could wait, I decided to try to track down Bailey. Just because she wasn't answering her phone didn't mean she wasn't around. Cell coverage was pretty spotty out at the park. The only reason my phone worked there was because it was ATAC-issue and pretty tricked out. Maybe Bailey was out in the wilderness somewhere with no signal. Probably telling the animals how great they were and how much people stank.

I bit my lip as I thought back on her comments earlier. She'd all but admitted she was trying to solve the case of the Misty Falls Lost herself. What if she'd found something? What if that was why she'd tried to call me?

Then again, maybe she wasn't trying to help at all. Frank and I had already wondered if Farley might have had an accomplice. What if that accomplice was Bailey?

Sure, she'd come right out to help look for

Frank. But now that I thought about it, she was the one who'd been doing most of the tracking. What if she'd purposely led us astray?

"At least this time I have a last name," I murmured as I texted a quick message to HQ.

They got back to me before I finished my second cup of coffee. Apparently Bailey wasn't too hard to research.

SUSPECT PROFILE

__Name:__ Bailey Cooper

__Hometown:__ Currently lives and works in Misty Falls State Park

__Background:__ Was born in a suburb of Pocatello, Idaho, but was orphaned at age five. Spent the rest of her childhood in foster care, mostly in or near Boise. Earned a scholarship to college, where she studied wildlife management and related subjects. Has worked in Idaho's parks ever since.

__Physical description:__ 5'7", 140 pounds, brown hair, brown eyes

__Occupation:__ Park ranger

Suspicious behavior: Seems to disagree strongly with Farley's ideas about the Misty Falls Lost; claims to be investigating the case herself.

Suspected of: Being involved in the disappearances and trying to cover it up; possibly being in cahoots with Farley O'Keefe; possibly killing him to protect herself or for other reasons.

Possible motives: Wanting to protect animals; acting out some childhood trauma of her own; other unknown motives.

Most of the info ATAC turned up I already knew or could have guessed. All except the stuff about Bailey being orphaned at age five. That was about the age of several of the abductees. Was there a connection?

I tried calling Bailey again. Still no answer, either on her cell or at the ranger's station. I sighed with frustration.

Just then a uniformed police officer strolled into the cafeteria. I recognized him as one of Rich's guys—he'd been helping search the campsite earlier.

"Hey, did you guys find anything?" I asked, hurrying toward him.

"Oh, hi, Joe. Sorry, no luck yet. Most of the guys are still out there, though. I just went off duty and came to check on Kurt on my way home."

"You're off duty?" I shot him a grin. "Okay, then I hate to ask. But I'm stuck here without a ride. Can you drop me off at the park?"

"Sure thing. Just let me grab a cup of joe." The cop hurried over to the coffee machine with me right behind him. "You going back to the campsite?"

I hesitated. I did want to see if anything was happening out there. Then there was Bailey—I still needed to track her down and find out why she'd tried to call me, especially given my new suspicions.

But first there was something else I wanted to check out. "Can you drop me at Farley's cabin?" I said.

The cop looked surprised but nodded. "Ready to go?" he asked, popping a lid on his coffee cup.

Fifteen minutes later I was ducking under the yellow police tape draped across Farley's doorway. There were still several hours of daylight left, but it was shadowy and dim inside thanks to the tall trees surrounding the cabin. With the crime scene tape hanging everywhere like huge cobwebs, the place was kind of creepy.

"Chill out," I muttered to myself. I'd been letting this park—and all the crazy stories about it—spook me way too much. It was time to channel Frank again and start being logical.

I poked around a bit, not quite sure what I was looking for. Anything suspicious. Anything showing that Farley and Bailey knew each other better than she let on. Anything that might tell me where to look for Frank.

I knew it was a long shot. But ATAC had taught us to follow up on every lead. Besides, I didn't have any better ideas.

There was a small, cluttered desk in the main room. A calendar was sitting atop a stack of papers. I peered at the notes scrawled all over it, but couldn't make heads or tails of them. If Farley had written them, the guy had seriously bad handwriting.

I tried to turn on a lamp to get a better look, but nothing happened. Great. Farley had only been dead for, like, twenty-four hours. Had the power really been cut off already?

Pulling out my phone, which had a pretty snazzy camera built in, I carefully snapped several photos of the calendar. I sent them straight off to HQ. Let the handwriting experts there figure it out.

"It's probably just Farley's notes about what he had for dinner," I muttered as I stuck the phone back in my pocket. "The guys will rib me about that for sure. . . ."

I let my voice trail off. Was I going crazy, or had the floor behind me just creaked?

"Hello?" I said, spinning around.

The room had gotten even darker since I'd come in. I peered around. Nothing moved.

CREAK!

There it was again! This time the sound came from around the corner.

I hurried that way, all my senses on the alert.

"Is someone there?" I called out in my best tough-guy tone. "Identify yourself!"

Silence. If there was someone in the cabin with me, he didn't want me to know it.

I spun around as a soft shuffling noise came from somewhere behind me. Digging into my pocket, I pulled out my ATAC-issue flashlight. I aimed the beam in the direction I thought the sound had come from. But the only thing I caught in its beam was a chair. Plus, the bright but narrow light made it even harder to see the rest of the room. Anyone—or anything—could be lurking in one of those shadowy corners. . . .

Before I could figure out what to do next, there

was a flare of headlights outside. My heart pounding, I rushed to the front door and saw Rich's cruiser pulling to a stop in front of the cabin.

"Joe!" the detective called out the open car window. "There you are—Marcus said I might find you here."

"You found me," I said, hurrying out to the cruiser. "What's up?"

Rich's face looked grim in the fading daylight. "It's Justin," he said. "He disappeared again."

Asking Alice

"W here are we, Alice?" I asked the little girl on the other side of the door. "What is this place?"

She shrugged, seeming disinterested in my questions. "Do you know where my brother is or not?"

"I'm not sure," I hedged. "Maybe he's with Luke. Do you know where Luke is?"

She frowned. "He's not with Luke! Don't be silly."

Interesting. It sounded as if she knew who Luke was.

"Are you sure?" I said, hoping for more information. I pressed my face against the window, watching her carefully. "Where *is* Luke, Alice? Can you tell me?"

"Uh-oh, guess you're still too forgetty," Alice said with a loud sigh. "But you came from the outs, right? Did you see my brother there? His name is Lee. I'm afraid he's lost!"

Her lower lip was starting to quiver. Uh-oh. If she started crying, I'd never get any useful information out of her. Plus, I hate seeing little girls cry. Or big girls, for that matter. It makes me nervous.

It was time to try another tack.

"Oh, *Lee* is your brother?" I said in what I hoped was a cheerful voice. Not easy to pull off under the circumstances. "Why didn't you say so? I know exactly where he is!"

Alice gasped. "Really?" she cried.

"Uh-huh. If you let me out of here, I'll take you to him."

Okay, I felt like a world-class schmuck lying to a little girl like that. But what other choice did I have? Besides, I figured if I could get us both out of here—wherever "here" was—she'd definitely be reunited with that brother of hers soon enough.

"Let you out?" Alice echoed, sounding uncertain. She stared at me for a second, then looked up and down the hall. "Um, I guess if you really know where Lee is . . ."

She reached toward the door.

BZZZZZZ!

A loud buzzer sounded overhead. With a squeak of terror, Alice jumped away from the door.

"Alice!" I called.

But it was too late. She was scurrying off down the hall without a backward glance.

I banged both fists on the door in frustration. So close, and yet so far!

Then I wandered over and collapsed on my cot, thinking about what had just happened. Okay, so I was still stuck in this cell. But at least I had a little more information.

It seemed Justin wasn't the only lost kid who was still around all these years later. Alice was here, and probably Luke, too. But where *were* we?

It was easy to guess why I was being held, even if I still didn't know why Alice and the others had been taken. Whoever had nabbed those kids must have thought Joe and I were a threat to whatever they were doing here. If only they'd known we'd still had pretty much no clue what was going on . . .

CLANG!

The door swung partway open again. I leaped to my feet, ready for anything.

An enormous, beefy young man stepped in. He had a round face and short, greasy hair. He was holding something in one hand. I winced as I recognized what it was. A taser.

He brandished it threateningly in my direction. "So you're the new one, eh?" he said in a slow, disinterested drawl. "Kind of old. Guess the Big Bossy B is branching out."

He seemed to crack himself up with that comment. Laughter spurted out of him, along with a few snorts and sniffles.

"Who are you?" I asked him.

He ignored me. "Guess you weren't hungry, eh?" he said with a glance down at the untouched tray of food.

I watched him carefully, looking for my opening. The door was still ajar behind him, and this guy didn't look too agile. If I could dart past him and avoid that taser . . .

"Yo, Baby Doc!" a different voice barked impatiently from the hallway. "Hurry up. We still got four more dinner trays to pick up before we can go off duty."

That changed things. Even if I could get past the first guy, I'd have to deal with at least one more outside in the hall.

Before I could figure out what to do, the big guy grabbed the tray and scurried out. The door clanged shut behind him.

I was still trapped. And I still had no idea what was going on here. But I was starting to feel like I was putting some puzzle pieces together. Now I knew it was probably evening—dinnertime. And that there seemed to be at least a couple of shifts of people working in this place.

"But what *is* this place?" I murmured under my breath. "Why'd they want all these kids?"

If only I could get out of this room, maybe I could figure out the answer to that.

I spent the next half hour or so trying to come up with a plan. Various buzzers and other noises came out of the speaker, but since they meant nothing to me, I did my best to ignore them.

Then the light blinked off, leaving me in total darkness once again. A few seconds later, tinny music tinkled out of the speaker. It took me a second to place the tune.

"It's a lullaby," I muttered.

Weird.

I lay down on my cot, arms propped behind my head. Staring up into the darkness, I kept pondering my situation. At least for a while.

I must have dozed off at some point. Because when I heard a soft, scraping noise somewhere nearby, I awakened with a gasp.

"Who's there?" I hissed, straining to see in the darkness.

And this time I could. See, that is. That's because

it wasn't pitch-black anymore. The door was opening, allowing a gray dimness into the room.

I jumped to my feet, all senses on alert. The door was still sliding slowly open. This time I wasn't going to let it shut me in again without a fight. . . .

Just as I was about to throw myself against the door, ready to take on however many men were out there, a small figure appeared in the opening.

"Alice!" I exclaimed. "Is that you?"

"Shh!" she hissed. She darted into my cell, casting a nervous glance behind her. She clicked on a small flashlight, aiming it straight at me so I had to shade my eyes. "I came so you can take me to see Lee. But we'll be in big naughties if anyone finds out we broke the schedule!"

I wasn't sure what that meant. But this didn't seem like the time to discuss it.

"Don't worry," I whispered in what I hoped was a reassuring tone. "Nobody will find out. Come on, let's go."

She nodded, turned off her light, and darted back out through the door. Taking a deep breath, I followed her out into the hallway.

Scene of the Crime

"Please, everyone. Let's just calm down and try to figure out the next steps." Rich let out a heavy sigh. He looked tired.

And no wonder. It was almost ten p.m., and it looked like there wouldn't be much rest for anyone tonight.

Justin was still missing. I'd gone along to help Rich search his room at the hospital earlier. But we hadn't found anything too useful. The obvious escape hatch was the room's wide-open window.

Then we'd had a few hours' break. I'd called into ATAC HQ to let them know how the search for Frank was going. Or *not* going.

I'd also moved my stuff into a local B and B.

Rich had set that up for me. For some reason, he didn't think it was a good idea for me to keep camping solo out at the park. Go figure. I certainly wasn't about to argue.

Still, I couldn't help feeling a little guilty about it. Like I was abandoning Frank. Leaving him out there somewhere on his own.

I tried not to worry about that. After all, I wouldn't be much help to him if I was eaten by a bear. Or nabbed by whoever had taken him.

Still, I was glad for the distraction when Rich called to see if I wanted to ride back to the hospital with him. First we'd checked on Officer Donnelly. Still out. Now we were standing around in the waiting room talking about how to proceed.

Dr. Carrini had turned up when he heard we were there, along with Dr. Hubert, Justin's primary doctor. Justin's mother, Edie, and her husband, Hank, were there too. They'd gone back to Boise to spend time with their other kids. But they'd rushed back to Misty Falls as soon as Rich had called them about Justin's latest disappearance.

"Where could he be? Why would he run away again?" Edie sobbed. "Was it because we left?"

Hank put a protective arm around her. "Don't blame yourself," he said. "We have kids at home who need us too. Justin understood that. He knew you were coming back soon."

Dr. Carrini nodded. "I doubt his leaving now had anything to do with you," he told Edie.

I winced. Tactful much? Still, the doctor's bedside manner was the least of my concerns at the moment.

"This just isn't fair!" Edie choked out between sobs. "Just when we'd found Justin again . . ."

Hank tried to comfort her. But it didn't work. She wouldn't be consoled.

Carrini noticed it too. "There, there," he told Edie. "You won't do yourself or Justin any good getting needlessly distraught. Why don't I give you something to take the edge off?"

That made Edie stop crying for a second. She stared at the doctor.

"You mean drugs?" she said, sounding indignant. "No, thank you!"

Dr. Carrini frowned, looking annoyed. "Fine. It's your choice, of course," he said in a stiff, offended voice. "But I don't know why so many people are so opposed to drugs that could help them! It's completely illogical."

"All right, then." Rich cleared his throat. "Let's just—"

Before he could finish, there was a sudden commotion of shouting voices and running footsteps from down the hall. A moment later Jacob Greer burst in. His girlfriend, a pretty younger woman named Donna McCabe, was right behind him.

To say I was surprised to see him was an understatement. The dude had taken off for Chicago just the previous morning, claiming he couldn't deal with the whole Justin situation anymore. He'd been pretty worked up about it, from what I'd heard. If anyone was responsible for Justin's sudden departure, it was a lot more likely to be Jacob than Edie.

Everyone else looked startled too. "Jacob!" Edie exclaimed. "You're back!"

Jacob ignored his ex-wife, turning right to Rich. "We took the first flight we could get from Chicago," he said breathlessly. "Is he back yet?"

Rich shook his head. "'Fraid not."

"Never mind," said Jacob. "We're ready to do whatever it takes to find him again. Cost is no object. In fact, I've already arranged for a top-notch private investigator to fly in from California."

"Uh, I see." Rich sounded a little confused.

I knew how he felt. Was this really the same Jacob Greer who'd stalked out of here just thirty-six hours ago or so? Talk about a major change of attitude! It seemed more than a little suspicious.

Jacob had been one of our only suspects until he'd left town. Was it time to put him back at the top of the list?

SUSPECT PROFILE

<u>Name</u>: Jacob Greer

<u>Hometown</u>: Doddsville, Idaho; currently lives in Chicago, Illinois

<u>Physical description</u>: 5'10", shaggy salt-and-pepper hair, brown eyes. A little heavy, rough around the edges

<u>Occupation</u>: Sporting equipment salesman

<u>Background</u>: Justin's adoptive father; ex-husband of Edie; currently in a relationship with Donna.

<u>Suspicious behavior</u>: Went from refusing to accept Justin as his son to loudly proclaiming his intention to do "whatever it takes" to find him.

<u>Suspected of</u>: Being involved with his son's latest disappearance, and possibly the first as well, and now trying to throw suspicion off himself.

<u>Possible motive</u>: Protecting himself from some family secret Justin might reveal?

"The PI should be here sometime tomorrow," Donna piped in brightly. "He's really very good. My family swears by him."

"Yeah." Jacob sounded impatient. "But we don't want to sit around twiddling our thumbs until he gets here. What's the plan, Detective Cole?"

"My men are still searching the hospital grounds," Rich replied. "If they haven't found any sign of Justin by morning, we—"

"By *morning*?" Jacob interrupted. "Are you nuts? I'm not going to waste time waiting on them. Has anyone searched the park yet?"

"The park?" I echoed.

"Yes, the park," Jacob said in an I'm-dealing-with-idiots voice. "That's where he supposedly was all this time, right? What if he went back there?"

"Mr. Greer, Misty Falls State Park is thousands of acres," Rich said. "There's no way we—"

"You don't have to search all of it," Jacob broke in impatiently. "Why not start with the obvious?"

"Which is?" Rich raised an eyebrow.

"The campsite," Jacob barked out. "Spot where some scum yanked him away from us the first time for who knows what reason. You know—scene of the crime."

Edie let out a muffled sob. "Jacob, please!" she wailed.

Dr. Carrini rolled his eyes. Hank looked anxious as he patted his wife on the back.

But Rich just shrugged. "S'pose it wouldn't hurt to go out there and take a look around." He shot me a look. "Want to tag along, Joe?"

"Sure," I said.

I had a feeling Rich was just humoring Jacob, trying to shut him up before he sent poor Edie into a nervous breakdown. I seriously doubted they were going to find Justin at that campsite. But you never knew. Besides, I wanted to keep an eye on the new and improved Jacob, and maybe take another look around for clues about where Frank had gone while I was at it. Not that I was expecting to find much at this time of night.

Edie and Hank decided to stay behind. Probably a good call. Edie was looking so upset by now that I was wondering if she hadn't been too hasty to turn down Dr. Carrini's offer of a little pharmaceutical assistance.

"We'll stop at the ranger station on the way in," Rich said as the four of us—me, him, Jacob, and Donna—climbed into his cruiser. "Let whoever's on duty tonight know where we're going. Just in case."

I shuddered, the image of that grizzly bear flitting through my head. And then that rattler. But

I pushed all that aside. There was safety in numbers, right? Besides, Rich was armed. And judging by the way he'd dispatched that deadly snake this morning, he was a pretty crack shot.

When we reached the ranger station, all the lights were on. The sounds of a radio playing country music drifted out through the open windows.

We climbed out of the cruiser and headed inside. It was a small place, just two rooms—a larger one with a desk and lounge area and a smaller one off to the side with a bunch of pamphlets and a few tanks with various species of local wildlife on display inside. There was nobody at the front desk when we stepped in.

"Hello?" Rich called. "Bailey, Michael, anyone here? It's Rich Cole!"

No answer. "Maybe they—," I began.

I was interrupted by a scream. It was Donna. She was staring into the side room. Her face was white.

"What is it, honey?" Jacob asked, hurrying toward her.

She pointed with a trembling finger. "Th-there," she gasped out.

Rich and I traded a worried look. Then we both hurried forward so we could see into that room.

"Oh, man!" I exclaimed when I finally saw what

Donna had seen. A big glass display tank taking up most of one wall. The top was off, and someone was slumped halfway into it. Headfirst.

"Bailey!" Rich called out, rushing forward. He carefully reached into the tank and felt for a pulse. "She's dead," he reported grimly.

"Dead?" Jacob exclaimed. "But how?"

I didn't need to ask. I'd already seen the huge, hissing rattlesnake twisting itself around the ranger's lifeless arms and torso.

FRANK

9

ploring

I found myself standing in the featureless hallway I'd seen earlier. It wasn't that different from
my cell, actually. Bare cement walls. Tile floor.
No windows. The only light came from a few tiny
bulbs near floor level. Night-lights, I guessed.

"Hurry up," a soft voice urged. "We need to go
find Lee!"

I glanced down at the little girl. Alice. Now that
I got a better look at her, I noticed she was wearing
a super-frilly pink nightgown and goofy fuzzy slip-
pers shaped like unicorns, complete with a glittery
silver horn poking up from each slipper. Perched
atop her head was a sparkly toy tiara.

The outfit was a little odd even for a ten-year-old

girl. But not worth worrying about, I figured, all things considered.

"Come on, Alice," I whispered. "Show me the way out of here. Then we'll go find your brother."

Alice shot a nervous look up and down the hall. "The Boss Man will be mad if he sees us," she whispered. "He doesn't like it when we break the schedule."

"It's okay. He won't find out," I assured her.

Ding!

A bell chimed softly out of some unseen speaker. Alice jumped and let out a squeak. Then she burst into tears and raced away down the hall.

"Alice!" I hissed after her. "Wait!"

It was too late. She disappeared around a corner.

Oh, well. At least I was out. I took a few steps in the direction the little girl had gone, glancing into the doorways I passed. There were three of them. Each led into another cell just like mine. Except that they were unoccupied, their cots unmade and doors standing slightly ajar.

When I rounded the corner, there was no sign of Alice. Just another hallway with several more doors leading off of it.

I glanced into the first one, expecting another cell. But that wasn't what I saw. Not even close.

Stopping short in surprise, I took a step inside,

squinting for a better look. This room also had whitewashed cement walls and no windows. But it was much larger than my cell. Like, at least twenty times larger. In other words, huge.

It was lit by several blue and green night-lights shaped like various animals. By their dim glow, I saw what appeared to be some kind of playroom. Swings, slides, and other playground equipment were set up on soft rubber mats. There were even a couple of good-sized trees growing in huge pots.

Not sure what to think of that, I returned to the hallway and moved on to the next door. This one led into another large room. The night-lights in here were all pink and white. This place was also a playroom, but set up as a sort of fairy-princess land. A sparkly castle playhouse. Springy plastic horses with flowing manes. Pink and glitter everywhere. You get the idea. Alice's super-girly outfit would fit right in.

When I came back out into the hall, I noticed a bluish glow coming from the far end. Stopping to listen, I heard a soft buzz and some clicks coming from that direction.

Tiptoeing forward, I peeked carefully around the corner. It opened into a large area filled with cubicles, desks, and filing cabinets. A bank of monitors lined one wall, though I was a little too far away to see what they were showing.

The space appeared to be a combo office/security area. The lights were dim in here, too, with the computer screens offering most of that blue glow. There was nobody in sight. I took a cautious step forward. If I wanted answers to my questions about where I was, this seemed a good place to find them.

Then I stopped short as I realized the place wasn't totally deserted after all. A lone female figure was bending over one of the desks.

My eyes widened in surprise. Could that really be . . . ?

"Hey! You there!" someone shouted from behind me.

Whirling around, I saw an annoyed-looking young man rushing toward me. He was dressed in drab hospital scrubs and was pretty average-looking in every way except one—the huge, nasty-looking pink scar bisecting his face. Ouch. Whatever had done that had to have hurt.

"How'd you get out?" Scar Guy demanded irritably.

"Same way I got in. Through the door," I shot back.

Then I jumped at him, wrestling him back

against the wall before he could even think about reaching for a weapon. ATAC training. Always go for the element of surprise.

"Let me go!" the guy yelped, struggling to break free.

He landed a couple of kicks on my lower legs. But he was smaller than me, and I was feeling pretty confident. Maybe if I could overpower him and find some ID . . .

ZZZZZZZIP!

"Aaaaaah!" I screamed as a bolt of electricity shot up my spine, turning my insides to Jell-O. Fiery, painful Jell-O.

Even through the sudden fog of pain and confusion, I knew what had happened. Someone had just tasered me from behind!

"Whew! Thanks, Baby Doc," said Scar Guy as he twisted free of my now limp grasp. "I don't know how this one escaped, but he . . ."

There was probably more, but I didn't hear it. I'd just felt a prick in my still-tingling arm. Then the sensation of a needle sliding into me. Things immediately started to go fuzzy.

No! I thought weakly as everything went dim. *Can't . . . pass . . . out . . . or . . .*

I felt myself sink helplessly to the floor. After that, everything went black.

Nuts and Bolts

"**A**ny news?" I asked as I stepped into the Misty Falls police station the next morning.

Rich looked up from some paperwork on his desk. "Morning, Joe," he greeted me, looking tired despite the huge, steaming cup of coffee sitting beside him. "Hope you slept better'n I did."

"Not really."

Rich just nodded. "Bailey was DOA when we got her to the hospital," he reported. "Multiple untreated rattler bites. Docs figure she must've been dumped in that tank around lunchtime."

I gulped, feeling uneasy. That meant Bailey had died pretty soon after she'd tried to call me.

I pushed that aside. What was the point in what-ifs? All I knew for sure was that this meant another suspect crossed off the list.

"So the snake attack was definitely what killed her?" I asked.

"The snake *venom* was what killed her," said Rich. "If she'd been conscious and able to get to the hospital reasonably quickly, she almost certainly would've recovered. Rattler bites are rarely fatal these days. But the coroner also found she'd had a severe blow to the head. Her bad luck that nobody happened along until we got there."

"So someone knocked her out, then draped her over that tank, knowing the snake would finish her off." I shook my head grimly. "Think someone's trying to send a message?"

Rich shrugged. "Maybe. Or maybe that snake was just a convenient weapon. Maybe whoever did it didn't necessarily even want to kill her—just give her a warning."

I turned as I heard voices outside. The door swung open, admitting Jacob, Donna, Edie, and Hank. Donna was dressed in riding breeches and tall, shiny black boots.

Okay, that seemed a little odd. But I don't waste much time worrying about other people's fashion choices.

"Morning, all," Rich said, his gaze wandering

toward Donna's outfit. "What can I do for you? That PI of yours here yet?"

"He'll be along this afternoon," Jacob said. "In the meantime, we've arranged for the local mounted Search and Rescue group to come in and help us look for Justin."

"Oh?" Rich's eyebrows shot up so far they were almost lost under the brim of his cowboy hat.

All four of them began talking at once. The gist was, Jacob and Donna had been up half the night on the phone with the Search and Rescue people. They both had some riding experience and were planning to ride along with the group. Hank was going too.

"I wish I could come along," Edie said, wringing her hands. "I just get so nervous around large animals. I'm sure I wouldn't be much help."

"Don't worry about it," Jacob told her, his eyes glittering with eagerness. Or maybe lack of sleep. It was hard to tell. "We'll call and let you know if we find any sign of him."

"Good luck with that," Rich said. "Not much cell reception out in the wilds of the park."

I was staring at Jacob, feeling suspicious. Why did it feel like he was trying way too hard all of a sudden?

Still, I wasn't one to look a gift horse—so to

speak—in the mouth. While those SAR folks were looking for Justin, they might as well be looking for Frank, too.

"Mind if I tag along?" I spoke up. "If someone can rustle up a spare horse, that is."

Donna looked me up and down, seeming doubtful. "Have you ever ridden before?"

"Sure, lots of times," I lied. The truth was, I'd only been on a horse a handful of times. But how hard could it be? I had great balance and reflexes from riding my motorcycle everywhere back home. That thing had some *serious* horsepower. An actual horse shouldn't be a problem, right?

An hour later I was standing in the park's main parking lot, watching the volunteers unload their horses from a couple of big stock trailers. One of the volunteers walked over to me. She was a fifty-ish woman with bright blue eyes and skin the color and texture of old leather.

"You Joe?" she asked in the direct way people seemed to address each other out here in the West.

I nodded and stuck out my hand. "Joe Hardy. Thanks for letting me ride along. Which one's my horse?"

"My name's Rina Charles." The woman shook my hand, then turned to squint at the group of horses. "That's your mount over there. The bay horse with the white socks. Name's Filbert."

"Filbert?" I echoed dubiously. That wasn't the kind of name I'd been expecting. More like Thunder, or Duke, or Maverick. Something western and rustic.

I looked at the horse in question. He was standing beside one of the trailers, his head hanging low. His eyes and lower lip drooped sleepily. Once in a while his tail swished at a fly. Otherwise he might as well have been a statue.

"He's an experienced dude horse," Rina said. "He'll take good care of you. And don't worry, he can keep right up with the younger horses once he works the kinks out."

That didn't sound too promising. I walked over to Filbert.

"Hey, buddy," I said, giving him a pat.

He opened his eyes slightly, then let them droop again. Otherwise, no response. Close up, he looked even more like a kids' pony ride horse.

"Um, are you sure this is the only horse available?" I asked another passing volunteer. "I mean, I was expecting something a little more, you know, spirited."

The second volunteer, a crusty cowboy-type dude who reminded me of Rich, shot me a suspicious look. "You the kid from out East?" he asked.

At my nod, he added, "Yeah, Filbert should do just fine for you."

Rina heard us and came over, looking slightly annoyed. "Look, you can ride along or not," she told me in a crisp, no-nonsense voice. "But if you're coming, you're riding Filbert, case closed. Mounted SAR work in the backcountry is dangerous enough without being overmounted. Especially for a novice."

"You sure Cole vouched for this one?" the man muttered.

I felt my face go red as Rina nodded. So that was why I was being allowed to ride along? Because Rich had put in a word for me?

In any case, I decided maybe it was better not to push it. Old Filbert would have to do if I didn't want to be left behind. So I shut up and tried not to attract any more attention to myself.

Soon we were setting off into the park. Rina led the way, mounted on an impressive-looking black horse. Jacob was right behind her on a stout chestnut. Then came Donna, the cowboy dude, and a couple of other volunteers, and then Hank. Filbert and I brought up the rear.

"Giddyup, boy," I said, swinging my legs against the horse's sides as we fell farther behind.

Filbert ignored me, ambling along at the same

relaxed gait. I wondered if he even remembered I was up there.

Oh, well. I might as well sit back and enjoy the ride.

About a mile in, we left the relatively clear trails and set out through the brush. It was pretty rugged country out there. Lots of rocks, lots of thorns, not much flat ground. Luckily, the horses seemed used to it, including Filbert. He wandered down steep, rocky hills and splashed through streams, never quite catching up to the other horses but never falling too far behind, either.

As for me? I was kind of surprised at how strenuous it was. I mean, Filbert was doing most of the work. All I had to do was sit there and hold on. But by the end of the first hour I was sweating, my leg muscles were screaming, and I was wondering when we were going to take a break.

Despite all that—and my worry about Frank—I couldn't help being awed by the park's natural beauty. There were no signs of civilization out here. Just deep canyons, rushing rivers, soaring hawks, ageless trees, and great views everywhere I looked. Beautiful, but definitely wild. A few times I found myself wondering what would happen if we got lost out here.

"Guess that won't happen, huh?" I murmured

to Filbert as we began another slow climb up out of another steep canyon. "I hear you horses can always find your way home."

Filbert flicked one ear back in my direction. Otherwise he didn't respond. He just kept climbing steadily up the twisting, narrow trail.

I gave him a pat, mentally apologizing for my earlier doubts. He might not be the swiftest horse in the world. But he hadn't put a hoof wrong on these tough trails. That was worth something.

Then I glanced forward. The rear end of Hank's horse was visible just cresting the top of the ridge. The rest were all out of sight already.

"Guess you were never a racehorse, were you, Filster old buddy?" I commented with a grin. "That's okay. Slow and steady wins the—"

I stopped short as I heard a weird whizzing sound somewhere right behind me. Was I being dive-bombed by a mosquito? I lifted my hand to swat at whatever it was.

At that same moment, Filbert snorted and jumped about a foot in the air, tossing his head skyward. I was so startled I started to slide sideways in the saddle.

I grabbed the horn to steady myself. Good thing.

Because a split second later, Filbert suddenly bolted off up the trail at breakneck speed!

Caring and Sharing

When I awoke to find myself back in my cell, I almost despaired. What *was* this place? How was I ever going to get out?

I closed my eyes to block out the harsh glare of the overhead light. My mind was feeling a little fuzzy again, though not nearly as bad as before. More like the typical getting-knocked-out kind of wooziness. I could deal with that.

So I did my best to focus. To try to make sense of what I'd seen on my brief trip out of my cell.

It wasn't easy. Nothing I'd seen made much sense.

But I was pretty sure of one thing: This was it. The place where all those missing kids had gone.

It had to be. The evidence all pointed to that.

Meeting Alice. Seeing Luke's name scratched into the wall. Those rooms full of playground equipment and other kid-friendly stuff.

I still had a lot of questions, of course. But one in particular.

Why?

Who would—and *could*—build a place like this? A secret place where a whole bunch of kids could be taken and never found?

And for what possible purpose?

From what I'd seen of Alice, she looked perfectly healthy. A little nervous, yeah. Obsessed with finding her brother, okay. But otherwise she'd seemed almost . . . normal.

Sort of like Justin. Yeah, he didn't seem to know how to use a knife or fork. And he came across as a little wild, a little untamed.

But he spoke perfectly good English. Could hold a conversation with people. Seemed pretty well-adjusted, all things considered. Was that because he'd been here all along, chatting with Alice and the others? If so, how in the world had he ended up wandering around Misty Falls with no memory of any of it—or of his own family, his own name?

CLANG!

I pulled myself together quickly. The little

window had just opened. Was it Alice? Had she returned to let me out again?

"Omigod!" a muffled female voice exclaimed. "I *thought* that was you!"

It wasn't Alice. But I definitely recognized the voice.

"I thought that was you I saw out there too," I said, looking into the pair of wide brown eyes staring down at me through the narrow window. "What're you doing here, Chloe? And where *are* we?"

I was already wondering if I was asleep and dreaming again. Why else would the cute, friendly candy striper from Mercy Hospital be in a weird place like this?

But I'd been pretty sure she was the person I'd seen out in that security area right before that goon tasered me. And now here she was.

The door cracked open just wide enough for Chloe to slip inside. She looked kind of upset.

"I can't believe you're here, Frank," she said, wringing her hands and staring at me. "Omigod, I really can't believe you're here!"

"Neither can I," I said. "Especially since I have no idea where 'here' is. Care to clue me in?"

If she heard the question, she didn't show it. "I can't believe it!" she repeated instead. "What was he thinking?"

"Who?"

She shot a nervous glance over her shoulder at the door. "Never mind," she said, lowering her voice. "What's done is done, I guess. I'm sure he has his reasons."

"Who does? Who's in charge of this place?"

"I probably shouldn't tell you." She tossed another nervous look at the door. "I mean, you'll find out soon enough anyway. But don't worry, okay?"

"Don't worry?" It was all I could do not to roll my eyes. "That's a little tough, given the circumstances."

She smiled briefly. "Yeah, I guess I can see that. But you've got to trust me, okay?"

"Trust you? What do you mean? What are you doing here, anyway?"

"I can't tell you that. Not yet," she said. "But please don't worry, Frank. You won't be hurt here. Nobody's hurt here." She hesitated. "Not on purpose, anyway."

Okay, *that* didn't sound too reassuring. My mind jumped immediately to that little girl whose bones had been found in the bear cave. Was that who Chloe was thinking about too? That everyone was safe here except the ones who happened to get accidentally fed to wild animals?

"What do you mean?" I asked again.

"The Big Boss means well, I promise," she said.

"The Big Boss? Who's that?"

"He only wants to help people. That's the whole reason for this place!"

"*What's* the whole reason?" I said. "What *is* this place? Where are we? Are we still in Misty Falls?"

She shrugged. "I'm sure he'll tell you all that if he thinks you need to know. But it doesn't matter. The important thing is, you're safe here."

Frustration bubbled up inside me. But I tamped it down. Chloe seemed to know all about this place. All I had to do was convince her to share.

"So this boss guy wants to help people, huh?" I said. "Okay. But how's he going to help me by keeping me here against my will?"

"I don't know." Uncertainly crept into her voice and eyes once again. "I'm sure he has his reasons, though. He always does."

"But why me? I'm just an innocent college kid writing a paper, remember?" I said, hoping she'd bought into my cover story. "And my brother will be super worried about me."

"I know. That's why I was so surprised to see you here." She bit her lip and gazed at me uncertainly. "I wonder if—"

DING!

A bell chimed urgently out of the speaker on the ceiling. A second later there was a crackle of feedback.

"Chloe," an expressionless computer-generated voice said. "Please report to the Caring Room. Chloe, please report to the Caring Room at once. Thank you."

The speaker clicked off. Chloe let out a squeak of terror.

"Chloe, wait!" I jumped to my feet.

But I was too late. She dashed for the door and slipped out, slamming it shut behind her.

More Mysteries

"**W**hoa!" I yelled as Filbert careened up the steep trail.

Hank heard me and glanced back. His eyes widened.

I braced myself, sure that Filbert was about to crash right into the other horse. But he didn't. He skidded to a halt with a few feet to spare.

Oof! I was flung forward by the sudden stop, and the saddle horn caught me right in the gut. But I stayed on.

"Joe!" Hank exclaimed. "Are you okay?"

There was a moment of commotion. We all stopped at the edge of the canyon. Now that it was over, my whole body was shaking.

Rina swung down from her horse and hurried toward me. She looked annoyed.

"What's going on?" she demanded. "Did you do something to make Filbert run? That's very dangerous on trails like these!"

"No kidding," I said breathlessly. I was still sort of collapsed over the saddle horn trying to recover. Filbert ducked his head to nibble on some tufts of dried-out grass.

The other volunteers were muttering to one another. Rina put her hands on her hips and glared.

"I had my doubts about you, young man," she snapped. "But I never expected this. Let's just hope Filbert didn't hurt himself, or it'll be a long walk back for you."

"But I didn't do anything!" I protested. "I was just sitting there, and he kind of jumped in the air and then took off like a shot!"

"Good old Filbert?" One of the other volunteers barked out a laugh. "Yeah, right. That horse wouldn't spook and bolt if his tail was on fire!"

Rina was already looking over the horse. She checked Filbert's bridle, then started running her hands up and down his legs, one at a time. Filbert himself seemed pretty unconcerned. He took a step forward, searching for more grass.

"He seems okay," Rina said at last, straightening

up and giving the horse a pat on the rump. "Lucky for you. But from now on, you'd better—hang on, what's this?"

"What's what?" Jacob asked. He glanced at his watch, looking impatient.

Donna steered her horse, an alert-looking Appaloosa, to the front of the pack. "Let's get moving, shall we?" she said in a voice that expected to be obeyed. "We've got a lot of ground to cover if we want to have any hope of finding Justin out here."

Rina ignored them both. She was peering at the back of my saddle.

"What is it, Rina?" one of the other locals asked.

"BBs," Rina said, sounding surprised. "There are a couple of BBs embedded here in the cantle of Filbert's saddle. Someone must have taken a shot at you!" She turned to stare at me.

"That makes sense," I said. "I heard something before Filbert took off. Could've been a BB shot."

Several of the other riders looked uneasy. "A BB gun?" one man said. "Who'd be way out here shooting at horses?"

Rina had turned to look over Filbert's hindquarters and side. "I don't see anything here," she said, sounding relieved. "And the BBs didn't go very far into the leather. I'm guessing the shooter was far enough away not to break skin."

"At least not a horse's skin," I said, glancing down at my own bare arms.

Rina rubbed her face and glanced at me. "Looks like I owe you an apology, Joe," she said. "This certainly explains why Filbert spooked. Any horse would if it got shot in the rump! Nothing to do with you. I'm glad you held on and weren't hurt. Sorry for jumping to conclusions."

"That's okay, no hard feelings," I said.

I scanned the walls of the canyon and the wooded areas on either side. There were plenty of places out here for a shooter to hide. And little chance we'd ever find him.

"So now what?" Hank sounded nervous. He probably wasn't used to being shot at back in suburban Boise. By BB guns or otherwise.

"Maybe we should head in," one volunteer said.

"Are you kidding?" Jacob sounded annoyed. "If someone's shooting at us, it must mean we're getting closer."

Donna nodded. "Maybe it's even Justin himself!" she said. "He might not realize it's us coming to help him."

On the one hand, I knew how they felt. My brother was out here too. If there was any chance of finding him, I wanted to press on.

On the other hand, we'd just been shot at.

Ambushed. By person or persons unknown.

Not a good situation to be in. Especially miles from civilization.

Okay, maybe it could be local kids playing a prank. But that seemed pretty unlikely. All my ATAC instincts told me those BB shots had to be a warning. What would happen if we didn't heed it? Would our attacker try again—and maybe not with a BB gun this time?

I glanced at Rina. She was staring up at the sky off in one direction. When I followed her gaze, I saw what she was looking at.

Storm clouds. Big, dark, angry-looking ones gathering on the horizon.

"Looks like some weather's rolling in," she said.

Right on cue, thunder rumbled in the distance. Everyone turned to look at the clouds.

"Looks like a bad one," someone said.

"That settles it," said one of the other volunteers. "We're heading in."

"What?" cried Jacob.

Rina was already turning her horse back the way we'd come. "We'd better hurry if we want to beat the rain back to the trailers."

Jacob and Donna kept protesting. But the locals all ignored them, following Rina.

I glanced at Hank. He stared back at me and

shrugged. He actually looked sort of relieved.

I knew how he felt. The park was beautiful. But also a little intimidating. Riding through it like this had given me a better idea of how vast it was. How untamed. The idea of finding someone out here just by riding along on horseback seemed crazy.

I mean, maybe that kind of thing worked for lost hikers and such. At least sometimes. But those people *wanted* to be found.

In any case, we didn't have much choice. Rina and the others were already heading down the trail back into the canyon. I tugged at my reins, turning Filbert so he'd follow them. This time, I hoped we'd make it through without getting shot at.

We retraced our steps, moving faster than we had the first time. Filbert even broke into a bouncy trot several times.

Even so, it was starting to spit rain by the time we reached the parking lot. Rina and the others worked fast, yanking off saddles and rushing the horses into the trailers.

Jacob and Donna didn't stick around to watch. They rushed off to their rental car and took off without a backward glance.

Hank and I stayed until the horses were loaded. Hank politely thanked the volunteers for their efforts, then turned to me.

"Need a lift back to town?" he asked.

"Yeah. Thanks."

It was raining hard by the time Hank dropped me off at the B and B. I raced for the door, but ended up drenched anyway.

There was nobody in the parlor that served as a lobby. Good thing. They probably wouldn't like me dripping all over their oriental rugs.

Pulling out my phone, I called Rich. He already knew about the aborted SAR mission. Jacob and Donna had stopped by the station on their way back to the park. They were staying at the lodge there.

"That fancy PI of theirs is due any minute," Rich told me. I could almost hear him rolling his eyes over the phone. "Guess they're planning to wait for him and show him around or what have you."

"Any other news?" I asked.

"'Fraid not. Justin's still missing. Edie's still upset."

"What about that kid from the hospital?"

"Stanley?" The detective sighed. "No change there, either. He's sitting in jail and still won't say who he is or why he wanted to talk to Justin."

I sighed, feeling frustrated. And worried. The investigation seemed to be going from bad to worse. With each passing minute, the chances of finding Frank seemed to fade.

"Okay," I said into the phone, trying not to sound as freaked out as I felt. "Keep me posted."

"Will do."

After I hung up, I just stood there dripping for a minute. Then I checked my watch. Almost two o'clock. That explained my grumbling stomach.

I decided to change into dry clothes, then grab lunch. Maybe a little nourishment would help my brain kick into gear and come up with a new plan.

Heading for my room, I fiddled with the key. But the door swung open as soon as I touched it.

Weird. Had I forgotten to lock up when I left that morning?

It was possible. I'd had a lot on my mind. But I was on alert as I stepped inside.

All was quiet in there. I scanned the room, looking for anything odd or out of place.

Then I saw it. A sheet of paper lying on the bed.

Hurrying forward, I grabbed it. It was a note made out of letters clipped from a newspaper. My eyes widened as I read it.

WE HAVE YOUR BROTHER. IF YOU DROP YOUR INVESTIGATION OF THE MISTY FALLS LOST, WE WILL GIVE HIM BACK.

IF NOT, YOU WILL NEVER SEE HIM AGAIN.

Food for Thought

CLANG!

I looked up from my spot on the cot. The cell door swung open. First I saw a tray of food pushed through the opening. Then the person carrying the tray.

"Chloe," I said.

"Hi, Frank." She smiled at me as she slipped inside. "I talked Jackson into letting me deliver your lunch today. We got interrupted earlier, and I wanted to explain."

"Explain what?" I sat up straighter. "Why I'm being held here against my will? And nobody will even tell me what's going on?"

She sighed and set the tray down on the cot.

"You're mad," she said. "I guess I don't blame you."

"You guess?"

Joe always says I'm no good at talking to pretty girls. Maybe he's right. But at the moment, I wasn't even aware of Chloe's appearance. Her silky dark hair. Or her soft brown eyes and dimpled cheeks. The way she smelled—like flowers in a meadow.

Okay, Frank, focus. I wasn't Joe, who gets distracted by any female who passes by. Besides, I had much more important things on my mind.

"So talk," I told her. "Explain away."

She perched on the cot. The tray was between us. She pushed it toward me.

"Go ahead and eat while we're talking," she urged. "I don't mind. And the guys will be back to pick up the tray in half an hour."

"I'm not hungry."

That was a lie. I was ravenous. How long had it been since I'd eaten anything? The food smelled delicious. This time it was a turkey sandwich. Lettuce, tomato, plenty of mayo. Plus a couple of chocolate chip cookies and another plastic cup of water.

But I didn't dare touch any of it. Not unless I wanted to risk passing out again. Losing more chunks of time. And maybe more of my memory.

I swallowed hard. My throat felt scratchy and dry. Very dry.

That was when I realized I could hold out for a while without food and be fine. But I probably couldn't go much longer without drinking. I'd have to risk the water. Picking it up, I took a few cautious sips.

It tasted fine. But who knew what could be hiding in it?

Chloe watched me drink. A worried little furrow creased her brow.

"I can't tell you everything," she said. "Not yet. But I can promise you that everything will be all right."

That seemed unlikely. At least as long as I was stuck in here. But I kept quiet, taking another sip of the water. It was helping clear my head a little already. Guess I hadn't even realized how thirsty I was.

"The Boss will explain it all to you soon," Chloe said earnestly. "Then you'll see that this place is really very special and good."

I set down the almost empty plastic cup. Then I glanced around at the bare walls.

"Yeah, this place is special all right," I said. "Kind of like prison is special."

She glanced around as well. "I know the Intro Cells are kind of grim," she admitted. "But I'm sure you'll be transferred to a regular room soon. I'll see what I can do to hurry that along, okay?"

"Regular room?" I said. "Is that where all those missing kids live? The ones who disappeared from the park?"

She shrugged and looked down at my tray. "Aren't you going to eat anything?" she wheedled. "Come on—just a few bites, for me? The cookies are really good here."

A few days ago, the way she was looking at me would have made me blush and stammer. Not now. If this was some twisted way to convince me to eat drugged food, I wasn't falling for it.

"Maybe in a few minutes," I said. "After you tell me what's really going on in this place."

"I told you, I wish I could." She tilted her head to one side, smiling uncertainly. "Please don't look at me like that—I'd tell you everything if I could. I swear."

You could tell me right now if you really wanted to, I thought.

But I didn't say it. It was obvious this interrogation wasn't getting me anywhere. Time to take a different tack.

"I know, Chloe," I said with a big, weary sigh. "Sorry for hounding you."

She brightened instantly. "That's okay," she assured me. "I know you're confused. Everyone is at first."

I nodded, biting back the urge to ask more questions. "Thanks for coming to talk to me," I said, pasting a big, earnest smile on my face. Joe calls it my Straight-A-Eagle-Scout look.

In the meantime, I was sneaking a peek toward the door. It was still standing slightly ajar. But Chloe was sitting between me and it. How was I going to get around her? She didn't look that tough or strong. But what if she had a taser hidden on her?

"Are you sure you don't want to eat something?" she said. "You should keep your strength up."

"Um, maybe you're right." I shot a look at the tray. "The trouble is, I'm allergic to tomatoes. I get a rash if I even touch one. Can you take them out of that sandwich for me?"

"Of course!" She bent over to pick up the sandwich.

That was all the break I needed. Pushing myself off the cot, I sprang toward the door. My legs felt a little wobbly after sitting around for hours, but I ignored that.

"Hey!" Chloe cried as I pushed past her. "Stop!"

I didn't stop. Dashing through the door, I turned and slammed it shut behind me.

A second later I heard Chloe pounding on the other side. "Let me out!" she yelled. "Frank, please! We'll both get in trouble!"

I wasn't too worried about that. As far as I could tell, I was in trouble already. Big trouble. But now maybe I could find my way out of it.

Ignoring the continued pounding and yelling, I headed down the hall. All my senses were on alert. I definitely didn't want to run into Scar Guy again. Or Baby Doc and his taser. Or anyone else, for that matter. Not until I figured out what was going on.

This time I went a different way than I had the first time. I found myself in a different featureless hallway. With different rooms opening off of it.

Two or three of the rooms had kids in them. A seven-year-old girl sitting on a plush pink rug eating a sandwich just like the one Chloe had brought me. A boy of around the same age sipping from his cup of water. Another boy, this one a few years older, working on some cookies while he sprawled on his bed reading a comic book.

Their rooms were much nicer than my cell. In fact, they were pretty much kids' dream rooms. Comfy, cheerful, loaded with toys. If not for the weird lunch trays and the complete lack of windows, the rooms could have fit right in at any suburban home.

Then I turned a corner and passed a different kind of room. A well-equipped laboratory. It was spacious and spotless, with shelves and tables full of test tubes, microscopes, and all sorts of other equipment I didn't recognize.

Right next door was another high-tech room. This one appeared to be a medical facility. Complete with an operating table. And every other piece of medical equipment you could imagine. The place was way fancier than anything I'd seen at the Misty Falls hospital.

"What *is* this place?" I murmured as I peeked in through the partially open door.

When I stuck my head in, I noticed a second operating table. It hadn't been visible from outside. Someone was stretched out on it. It was hard to see much in the dim light, but the figure was hooked up to an IV and lying very still.

I took another step in, peering at the figure. Then I gasped.

"Justin!" I whispered.

JOE
14

Smith Comes to Idaho

I stared at the note in my hand. "If you drop your investigation, we'll give him back," I murmured. Tempting. But only for a second.

For one thing, even if I did promise to drop the mission, what were the odds that they'd really return Frank? It was kind of hard to trust someone who would kidnap a bunch of little kids.

Besides, I knew Frank wouldn't want me to do it. No way. He'd want to keep on with our mission no matter what. An ATAC agent never gives up.

The thought picked me up. If someone was offering a trade, there was a pretty good chance that Frank was alive and well somewhere. All I had to do was find him.

No problem, right? Yeah, right!

I changed into dry clothes and tucked the note in my pocket. Then I pulled on a rain jacket and headed outside. Lunch would have to wait a little longer. I was planning to walk over to the police station to show the note to Rich.

Then I paused on the front porch. I stared out at the rain as a new thought occurred to me.

What if Rich was involved in this somehow?

Now that I thought about it, it made a crazy kind of sense. Rich was the only local who knew who Frank and I really were. Why we were there.

Him and whoever had left that note.

All the locals around here seemed to know one another from way back. Often with weird interconnections—like old Farley being Justin's grandfather.

So what if Rich had some secrets he wasn't sharing too? After all, he was one of the few people who'd known I was on that Search and Rescue ride. He'd made sure we stopped by the ranger station where we'd found Bailey's body. He'd known that Frank was at the campsite with just the one other cop.

Come to think of it, he'd been around for most of the suspicious stuff that had happened. Should Frank and I have been so quick to trust him?

Reaching into my pocket, I touched the note. Maybe I'd hold off this time, at least until I had a chance to think it over.

Maybe it was even time to put Rich on the suspect list. Just in case.

SUSPECT PROFILE

<u>Name:</u> Detective Richard Cole

<u>Hometown:</u> Misty Falls, Idaho

<u>Physical description:</u> 6'2", 245 pounds, 48 years old, thinning brown hair, hazel eyes. Rarely seen without his cowboy hat.

<u>Occupation:</u> Detective and sheriff of the Misty Falls Police Department

<u>Background:</u> Born and raised in the immediate area. Worked his way up through the department. Married with a daughter attending college in Montana.

<u>Suspicious behavior:</u> None in particular, but has had full access to the investigation all along.

ATAC got back to me quickly with Rich's info.
Again, he didn't seem too hard to research. I stared
at his bio, feeling uncertain about my new suspicions.

So I turned my thoughts to our other suspects.
Well, *suspect*—singular. With Farley and now Bai-
ley dead, the only decent suspect we had left was
Jacob Greer.

Plus maybe the kid in the jailhouse, Stanley
from Seattle. But that one seemed like a long shot.

So could Jacob be our guy? True, he couldn't
have been the one who'd taken a shot at Filbert
and me. But he could have had an accomplice.

I decided to head to the park and talk to him.
Luckily, the owner of the B and B returned just in
time to give me a ride over to the lodge. That was

one nice thing about Misty Falls. Most people there seemed more than willing to do you a favor.

The B and B owner dropped me off in front of the lodge. The parking lot was almost empty. That made it impossible to miss the awesomely tricked-out motorcycle parked in the handicapped spot right in front of the lobby entrance.

I couldn't help walking over to stare at it. Frank and I have some pretty nice bikes back home. We ride them almost everywhere we go, and they're probably the coolest things we own.

But this thing made ours look like kids' tricycles. I'm talking custom everything from handlebars to taillight.

Still, I had more important things to do than drool over a bike. Especially when all it did was remind me of Frank.

Turning away, I headed inside to find out Jacob's room number. But I didn't need it. Jacob himself was right there in the lobby. Donna was standing beside him with a big smile on her face and her arm tucked through his.

They were both talking to a tall man with slick, dark hair. He was wearing a suit and tie and expensive-looking sunglasses.

When I went over, I found out this was him. The bigshot PI from California.

"Mr. Smith is sure he'll be able to find Justin," Jacob said as he introduced us.

Mr. Smith? Yeah, right.

"Are you one of Justin's young friends?" Smith asked as we shook hands. His voice was as snooty and over-the-top as his look.

I shot him an innocent smile. "Something like that."

"Joe's got a special interest in this case," Donna put in. "His brother was taken the other night. Possibly by whoever's responsible for Justin's disappearances."

"Hmm." Smith looked me up and down. Then he turned away and flicked a spot of lint off his suit sleeve. "I suppose we should get started. Why don't you get me up to speed on this case?"

He sounded kind of bored. Jacob and Donna didn't seem to notice. They started filling him in on Justin's disappearance, reappearance, and latest disappearance.

"Seems simple enough," Smith said when they finished. "I'm sure we can wrap this up quickly, especially if the local yokels stay out of my way."

I winced. Smith's voice was pretty loud. At least loud enough for the lodge staff to hear him. Tact-tastic.

"Want to take a look at Justin's hospital room?"

Jacob asked. "Maybe talk to his doctors?"

Smith shook his head. "Let's start right here in the park. I want to see the spot where he first disappeared."

Jacob and Donna exchanged a confused look. "Where he *first* disappeared? Are you sure?" Donna asked.

"That all happened almost twelve years ago," Jacob added. "I can't imagine what you expect to find there after all this time."

But Smith was already striding toward the door. Donna put a hand on Jacob's arm.

"Come on," she told him. "Mr. Smith knows what he's doing."

Jacob looked ready to argue for a second. Then he shrugged and allowed her to drag him along.

I tagged along. So far I wasn't too impressed with Mr. Snazzy-Suit Smith, Super PI. But I was willing to be convinced. We needed all the help we could get on this case.

When I got outside, Smith was walking toward the motorcycle I'd been admiring earlier.

"Whoa, that your ride?" I said. "Nice sled!"

He shot me a smug smile. "Thanks," he said, climbing on. "Hard work has its rewards, my boy."

I waited until he turned away to roll my eyes. Yeah, I'd just met the guy, and he already annoyed me.

But if he actually found something, I didn't want to miss it. Especially if it might lead me to Frank.

I managed to invite myself along as Jacob and Donna climbed into their rental car. Smith followed on his bike, and we headed deeper into the park.

We started at their old campsite, just as Smith had ordered. Jacob seemed pretty uncomfortable being there. He wouldn't move more than a few steps from the car. Or look around much.

But Donna and I joined Smith as he wandered around the site for a while. He kept both hands in his pockets, kicking randomly at rocks and leaves and stuff.

I was getting less impressed all the time. "Um, what are you looking for, exactly?" I asked after a few minutes.

"It would take too long to explain to a layperson," he replied with a condescending smile. "Just be careful not to damage any evidence while you're wandering around."

Yeah, right. As if there was any evidence left after a dozen years. Even if there was, he'd be just as likely to mess it up as anyone, at least based on what I'd seen so far.

But I bit my tongue. I didn't want to get kicked

out of this investigation. If you could call it that.

After Smith finished at that site, we headed to a few others around the park. The spot where a girl named Kerry had gone missing the year after Justin. The parking lot where a boy named Luke had been snatched while sleeping in his parents' car. Jacob and Donna had been doing their homework. They knew them all.

Finally we ended up at our campsite. The one where Frank had disappeared. The tent was still there. So was the word LOST scrawled in the dirt, though it was kind of smudged thanks to the rain earlier that day.

I stared at it. It gave me the creeps.

Smith climbed off his bike. He'd ridden it all the way to the campsite, though the rest of us had left the car back at the parking lot and walked. The thing wasn't exactly built for off-roading. But since he only went about two mph, it didn't really matter.

"So what happened?" he asked me, sounding more bored than ever. "Your brother wandered off and disappeared?"

"Not exactly," I said. "It all started with the grizzly bear. . . ."

I told him the whole story. The bear. Me and Rich heading for the hospital. Coming back to find the other officer out cold and Frank nowhere to be seen.

When I finished, Smith looked skeptical. "You boys experienced campers?"

"What does that have to do with anything?" I asked.

He shrugged. "I'm just not convinced yet that your brother's situation is connected with Justin's disappearance. Of course, if you'd like me to look into it for you, I'm sure I could combine the cases for an appropriate supplemental fee. . . ."

Annoyance bubbled up in me. I tried hard not to let it show.

"Thanks for the offer," I said through clenched teeth. "I'll think it over."

Then I walked away. I was really getting tired of this guy's attitude. Who did he think he was? After what I'd seen so far, I'd hire my aunt Trudy as a private investigator first! At least she might be able to pass ATAC's novice-level training courses. Smith? Not a chance.

Smith started pontificating to Jacob and Donna as they wandered toward the tent. Leaving them to it, I started poking around on my own nearby. Yeah, I'd pretty much covered the area with Rich the day before. But what if we'd missed something? There had to be some clue. No way could Frank just disappear like that. Without a trace.

I was searching a wooded area near where Smith's bike was parked when I felt my cell phone buzz in my pocket. Pulling it out, I saw a new e-mail message. It was from ATAC HQ.

Frank! I thought with a flash of hope.

What if he'd managed to get in touch with them? Maybe they were writing to say he was safe and sound somewhere. . . .

As soon as I clicked open the message, my hope faded. Of course. They were responding about those photos I'd sent them. The ones of the scrawled notes on Farley's calendar. I'd almost forgotten about that.

Our handwriting experts have worked out most of the notes, the message read. *See transcribed messages below*—

I didn't get a chance to read any more. Something had just moved in the woods nearby.

My head snapped up as I scanned the area. I could barely hear the others talking; they were still over by the tent. At least thirty yards away.

Whatever I'd just seen was much closer.

A twig snapped. I spun around.

"Who's there?" I called out.

For a second I felt stupid. I shot a look back

over my shoulder. If the others heard me talking to some passing deer or squirrel . . .

SNAP!

My head spun back around. Just in time to see something dart behind a grove of trees. Something . . . or some*one*.

"Hey!" I called. "Is someone there?"

I was answered by the muffled roar of a motor. A second later an ATV shot out from behind the trees! "Stop!" I yelled.

The figure hunched over the handlebars ignored me and gunned it. The ATV went tearing off down the hill, farther into the woods.

I glanced around frantically. Smith and the others were nowhere in sight by now.

But something else was.

Smith's bike.

Rushing over, I vaulted aboard. The motorcycle roared to life beneath me, its powerful engine purring like a kitten. A very large kitten with some serious horsepower. And lots of teeth.

"Hey! What are you doing?" I heard Smith yell out from somewhere behind me.

But I ignored him. The ATV was already out of sight ahead.

Jamming the motorcycle into gear, I revved the engine and took off after it.

owhere to Run

I stared down at Justin, my head spinning with questions. His eyes were closed. He was lying very still. But I could see his chest rising and falling steadily.

Good. He was alive.

"Hey!" someone shouted from somewhere behind me. "What are you doing in there?"

I spun around. Scar Guy was hurrying down the hallway toward me. The big guy he'd called Baby Doc loomed behind him.

Darting out the door, I started to run in the opposite direction. I'd only gone a few steps when several more people appeared at that end of the hall. Three other young, strong, tough-looking dudes. A pretty brown-haired girl in her late teens. And Chloe.

Uh-oh. I was busted.

I glanced over my shoulder. Baby Doc was holding up his taser as he and his pal barreled toward me.

There was nowhere to run.

"Should I fry him, guys?" Baby Doc asked eagerly as they all reached me. He raised his taser.

"No!" Chloe cried.

Scar Guy held up a hand to stop the bigger man. "Hang loose, Baby Doc," he said. "I just talked to the Big Boss about this guy."

"You did?" Chloe glanced at him. "What'd he say?"

Scar Guy shot me a smile. It wasn't particularly friendly .

"Looks like Frank here will be a permanent guest in the compound," he said. "We're supposed to start his prep."

Chloe's mouth formed a little O of surprise. But Scar Guy ignored her, turning to the younger girl.

"Hey, Kerry, grab me a pair of gloves, okay?" he told her.

Despite my present situation, I couldn't help doing a double take when I heard the name. "Kerry?" I blurted out. "You're one of them! One of the Misty Falls Lost!"

Kerry had been the name of the second child to disappear, about a year after Justin. She'd been eight years old when she was taken. That had been nearly eleven years ago, which would make her about nineteen today.

She stared at me blankly. "What are you talking about?" she asked.

"Shut up, you." Baby Doc's beefy hand darted out, giving me a resounding slap on the head. Ow. The guy didn't need a taser to do some damage.

Chloe followed Scar Guy as he led the way into the medical room. Baby Doc wrestled me along behind them.

"Listen," Chloe said, sounding anxious, "are you sure about this? Frank's not like the other ones. He has people out looking for him, and from what I've heard in town I don't think they're going to give up. Or believe he got eaten by a bear, either."

Scar Guy just laughed. "Don't worry your pretty little head about it," he said. "The Boss will figure something out."

"Yeah," one of the other tough guys put in with a smirk. "And even if he doesn't, they'll never find us here. You know that, Chloe."

Scar Guy nodded. "I almost forgot," he told her. "The Boss wanted me to tell you—he wants Frank to be your special project. Says he thinks you're ready."

Chloe's eyes widened. "Really?" she said. "He really said that?"

"Uh-huh. So are you ready to get started?"

Chloe hesitated, shooting me an uncertain glance. Then she straightened her shoulders and turned back toward Scar Guy.

"I'm ready," she declared. "Let's get this done."

"Chloe!" I said. "What's going on? I thought we were, you know, friends or whatever."

She ignored me. Baby Doc's grip on my arm tightened, and one of the other guys helped him wrestle me farther into the room. Toward that second operating table.

I tried to protest. Kept fighting to get loose. But Baby Doc was scary strong. And nobody was paying attention to anything I said anymore.

Not even Chloe. She was pulling on a pair of latex gloves. Nearby, Kerry and Scar Guy were opening cabinets and bustling around.

To be honest, I wasn't too focused on them. I was paying a lot more attention to Baby Doc and the other guy. They dragged me over and hoisted me onto the table.

"Let me go!" I yelled, struggling for all I was worth.

It didn't do any good. Within seconds, they had me strapped down onto the table. My arms and legs were immobilized. Even my head was held in place by a wide strap.

I was helpless.

From that position, I couldn't see much. All I could do was strain to hear what they were saying. Figure out what was about to happen to me.

But they weren't saying much. Kerry murmured, "How many cc's?"

"Start with six," Chloe answered.

"You okay here?" asked Baby Doc. "It's almost time to pick up trays. Don't want to break schedule."

"Go ahead, and take Carl with you," Scar Guy said. "I'll stay and keep an eye on things here."

Then footsteps. Fading quickly.

A moment later Chloe appeared beside the table. She bent over me, smiling distantly.

"This won't hurt much," she assured me, not meeting my eye.

"Chloe, don't do this!" I struggled against my restraints. They held tight. "Please, just stop and think about what you're doing!"

The only sign she'd heard me was a small twitch of her lips. She tied a cuff around my bicep and inflated it, making my arm throb. Then I felt her gloved hand touch my skin just below the cuff.

"Chloe, please!" I whimpered.

Yeah, I said whimpered. Can you blame me? I was feeling helpless and hopeless. My mind raced, looking for a way out, but I couldn't see one.

Chloe kept her gaze on my arm. She reached for

something, and I felt cool liquid dab onto my skin.

"I'm about to insert the IV," she said in a flat, clinical voice. "Please hold still."

Yeah. As if I had a choice . . .

I felt the needle pierce my skin and slide into the vein. Just then Kerry appeared in my line of vision. She was pushing a tall metal IV rack. Hanging from it was a clear plastic bag filled with bright purple liquid. A tube ran down toward me.

"What's that?" I demanded. "What are you doing to me?"

"Hush," Chloe said soothingly as she finished inserting the IV and then reached for the tube. "This is all for the best. You'll see."

I felt the first globs of cool liquid pump into my arm through the IV. Chloe and Kerry stood there watching for a moment. Scar Guy appeared too, looking down at me.

I wanted to yell at them. To protest all this. But suddenly it just felt like too much effort. My eyelids started to droop.

"Looks good," Scar Guy said. "Let's leave him alone. It'll work faster if he's less agitated."

They all disappeared. I was vaguely aware of footsteps fading away, of the door clanging shut.

But I couldn't quite make myself care. I was just too tired. So tired . . .

Different Kind of Horsepower

S mith's bike had power to spare. If I'd been out on the highway, there was probably nothing that could have outrun it.

The trouble? I wasn't on the highway. I was in the middle of the dense, rocky, wooded, mostly untamed wilderness of Misty Falls State Park. In other words, *not* the ideal conditions for a road bike. No matter how massively awesome it was.

Still, it was all I had. I'd just have to make the best of it.

Calling on every ounce of experience I had, I managed to keep the bike upright as I shot down the hill after that ATV. It was already almost out of sight again along a narrow, rocky trail.

"Come on, baby," I murmured to the motor-cycle as I swerved around a boulder, almost skidding out on a patch of mud. "Don't let me down."

The bike's engine whined as I pushed it a little faster, keeping one eye on the trail, and the other on that ATV.

The guy was bent over the handles and really thrashing it. He—or maybe she, there was no way to tell—was dressed in a dark, billowy jacket and a helmet. It could have been anyone up there from what I could see.

Whoever it was could ride. And seemed to know where he was going. It took all my skills to keep him in sight while keeping the road bike upright.

I tore down a bumpy hill and through some underbrush. Soon my arms were bleeding from multiple scratches. But I hardly noticed. I couldn't let up, or I'd lose him!

The ATV rider made a sharp left up ahead. I sped up as much as I dared, only slowing down for the turn. The bike's tires slipped a little on the uneven ground. But I sat steady and steered through it.

Whew! That was close.

The ATV was just disappearing over the next rise. Crouching down, I gunned it after him.

We ripped it up for another twenty minutes or more. Uphill. Downhill. Through a shallow stream.

Was it my imagination? Or was I starting to gain on him?

My heart pounded. I pushed the bike a little harder. . . .

SKREEEEEEE!

"No!" I yelled, fighting to stay upright.

But it was too late. A patch of loose gravel had come out of nowhere! The bike's tires were skidding out but not slowing down.

"Aaaaaah!" I yelled as I saw a bunch of scattered rocks coming up fast.

I hauled on the handlebars. The bike tipped and wobbled. . . .

"Oof!"

I hit the ground hard, landing several yards from the bike. It was making a terrible clamor as it bounced and scraped across the rocks. Finally it somersaulted over a boulder and smashed to a halt against a huge tree trunk.

The echoes of the impact rang off the nearest canyon walls. When they faded, I heard the ATV again. Sounding farther away all the time.

Testing each of my limbs, I was relieved to find them all still in one piece. I climbed to my feet. My whole body was going to be a giant bruise tomorrow. But I was okay.

The bike? Not so much.

I stood it up and grimaced. Smith definitely wasn't going to appreciate the results of my horizontal parking job. Oh well.

Climbing on, I tried to get the thing started again. But no matter how I fiddled with it, I couldn't even get the engine to whimper.

I soon realized I couldn't even hear the ATV anymore. I'd lost it for sure.

Disappointment flooded through me. But that wasn't the worst of it. When I glanced around, I realized I had no idea where I was!

"Uh-oh," I murmured, squinting up at the sun. It was already sinking toward the horizon.

In all the excitement of the chase, I hadn't paid enough attention to where I was going. Just like Frank was always hassling me about. Oops.

At least the bike had left plenty of tracks. Leaving it where it was, I started retracing my steps. Or, rather, my treads.

It was already pretty shadowy beneath the trees. Before long, it would be too dark to see.

I pulled out my ATAC flashlight. Luckily, it hadn't been smashed in the wipeout. Using it helped a little. But it was slow going.

AROOOOOO!

Wolves! The howl was pretty distant. But still seriously creepy.

Maybe it was time to call for help. I grabbed my phone.

Just one problem. I couldn't get a signal. "Oh, man!" I murmured, trying again and again. This was a first. I'd thought my ATAC phone would have reception on the moon! But apparently not in the backwoods of Idaho. My wild ride must have taken me even farther from civilization than I'd thought.

"So now what?" I murmured, glancing around.

Smith might not care about me. But he'd want his bike back. Would he call the cops or the rangers to look for me when I didn't return? Or would he try to track me down himself?

Either way, I figured I was pretty much stranded. At least for tonight. There was no way I'd be able to hike out the way I'd come before dark. Not even close. If I tried, I'd be likely to stumble off the edge of some steep canyon. Or maybe walk right into the jaws of those wolves I'd heard.

Calling on my ATAC training, I decided it was time to set up camp. Hunker down, try to stay warm. Figure out what to do in the morning if nobody had found me by then.

There wasn't much daylight left by now. I hurried around gathering firewood. It wasn't easy to find enough dry tinder after that day's rains, but finally I had a decent blaze going.

By then it was almost fully dark. I sat down by the fire, warming my hands. It was warm during the day. But the nights up there in the mountains got chilly fast.

My stomach grumbled. I realized I hadn't eaten a thing since breakfast.

Our ATAC training had covered that kind of thing too. Roots and berries. Stuff that was safe to eat out in the wilderness. I thought about taking my flashlight and going in search of some.

But when I looked out at the darkness beyond the fire's warm glow, I couldn't do it. The nighttime noises were starting up. Chirping insects. Wolves and coyotes in the distance. Other sounds I couldn't place. Surrounding me, making me feel totally exposed sitting here all alone.

"There's no such thing as ghosts," I muttered, trying to channel Frank again.

It didn't work. Sure, my rational mind knew ghosts weren't real. But this place was pretty creepy. I decided I could deal with the hunger. At least until morning. The roots and berries would still be there when the sun came up again.

I curled up beside the fire, tucking my hands into my shirt for warmth. The red glow of my campfire danced behind my eyelids, and I could feel its warmth on my face. Finally I managed to doze off.

I awoke sometime later. My face was so hot I was sweating. For a second I wasn't sure where I was.

Then I remembered. I was stranded in the wilderness. At first I thought I'd rolled too close to my fire.

My eyes cracked open. A hot red glow lit the scene. But the campfire was right there in front of me. Nothing but embers.

I sat up fast, suddenly wide awake. The red glow wasn't coming from my fire. It was coming from the trees nearby!

"Forest fire!" I gasped out.

I jumped to my feet and stared around frantically. Everywhere I looked I saw dancing flames. A deadly inferno surrounded me on all sides.

I was trapped!

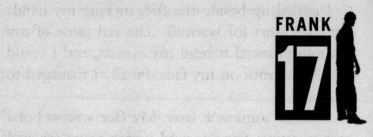

The Tunnels

Sleep pulled at me, dragging me down into darkness. Warm, comforting darkness. All I had to do was let go, to sink into its embrace, and then all my worries would be over. . . .

I was about to give in to the overwhelming weariness. Why shouldn't I? Suddenly I couldn't remember any good reason not to let go. Just let everything go . . .

Then I heard something. Footsteps. Rushing toward me. Forcing my eyes open, I saw a small face hovering over mine.

It was hard to focus. My eyes weren't really doing what I wanted them to do.

"No!" a voice cried.

I recognized that voice. Who was it?

Someone yanked the IV out of my arm. It hurt, but somehow that didn't seem to matter.

"A-Alice?" I mumbled with some effort as a name floated out of my jumbled mind.

I felt small hands poking at me. "Come on!" Alice hissed, her face still above me. "You said you'd take me to Lee. But if they give you the forgetting potion, you might not remember where he is!"

Lee. Who was Lee? I was feeling pretty fuzzy about all this. But then I felt the straps loosen from my arms and legs.

Escape. I could escape now. That was what I wanted. Wasn't it?

Yes. I was pretty sure it was. I slipped my head out from beneath its strap and sat up.

And almost fell over. Lights twinkled at the edges of my vision.

I did my best to blink them away. When I turned my head to look at Alice, the motion made me feel woozy.

"Come on!" she whispered.

I nodded. That made me feel woozy too. But I ignored it. Taking a few deep breaths, I swung my legs around and stood.

Sort of. I had to grab the edge of the table for

a second until the room stopped spinning.

Alice was already heading for the door. I staggered after her.

"I think I figured it out," she whispered. "It's this way."

I had no idea what she was talking about. But I followed as she dashed off down the hall.

Time passed. I was having trouble keeping track of it. Or of where we were going. We seemed to be passing through a lot of halls, making a lot of twists and turns. Once in a while we ducked into a room until somebody passed by outside.

One of those times I saw a little girl sleeping on a bed. At least I was pretty sure it was a bed. It was shaped like a giant panda bear.

Weird.

As we slipped back out into the hall, I started to wonder if I was really awake. Was this real life? Or was I stuck in another bizarre dream? I checked behind me, half expecting to see that grizzly bear come roaring around the corner.

Instead I heard footsteps. Alice gasped.

"Hide!" she whispered, pulling me into another room.

This time there was nobody inside. I looked around, but the lights were off and I couldn't see much. Just a few desks and chairs. Like a schoolroom. That seemed sort of important somehow. But I couldn't seem to focus on it.

Alice was peeking out again. "Come on, he's gone," she whispered.

I followed her back out into the hallway. My legs were working better now. But my head was still pretty hazy. I knew it was urgent that I get away from this place. But why? Where was I going?

"Joe," I blurted out. The image of my brother's face had just floated through my mind.

That was it! I needed to find Joe. Where was he? Had the wolves eaten him?

Wait. What wolves? I shook my head to clear it, realizing I was confusing dreams and reality again. . . .

"Aaaaah!"

A sudden yell came from somewhere nearby. Alice spun around, staring at a half-open door.

"Uh-oh," she said. "Sounds like a night-mem."

"What?" I said.

The door flew open. A little boy in pajamas burst into the hallway, waving his arms over his head. His hair was rumpled and his eyes stared wildly, not seeming to see us.

"I remember!" he shouted in a voice cracking with terror. "I remember it now! I remember!" By the end, the shout was more like a shriek.

"Hurry! In here!" Alice yanked me through a different doorway. We found ourselves in a utility closet. A water heater clanked away in the corner, and there were shelves filled with paper towels and such.

We huddled there, watching through a crack in the doorway as people came rushing from every direction. They converged on the screaming little boy.

A dark-haired man in a white coat grabbed the boy. "Relax, Kyle," he said in a calm voice. "We'll take care of you. Don't worry."

My eyes were doing weird things again. I couldn't seem to focus on the man. But his voice sounded familiar. Who was he? Was it the man with the scar? Or the big one, the one who'd tased me? I wasn't sure, but I didn't think so. . . .

Within moments, the little boy was back in his room. A few of the people went with him. The others wandered away.

As soon as the hall was empty, Alice dashed out of our hiding place. I hurried after her. We tiptoed around the corner. Another long hallway lay before us.

I sighed. Would we ever run out of hallways? Once again, I had the weird feeling of being in a dream. Running and running, with no hope of escape.

Then I realized Alice was speaking. "Huh?" I said.

"There it is," she hissed, jabbing one small finger at something farther down the hall. "The door to the tunnels!"

"The tunnels?" I echoed, feeling more confused than ever.

She frowned, giving me an impatient look. "The tunnels!" she whispered urgently. "Justin told me that's how he was going to get outside!"

"Justin . . . ," I mumbled. It took me a moment to remember who he was.

Oh, yeah. The kid back in the medical room. The one Joe and I had come to help.

I didn't have time to remember any more. Alice was on the move again. I followed her down the hall.

Then there was a shout. Alice let out a squeak and ducked through the nearest doorway.

This time I was almost too slow. I barely made it in behind her before someone stomped into view at the end of the hall.

"Anybody home?" a loud voice shouted.

Even though he was shouting and stomping, he didn't sound angry. He sounded kind of pleased with himself, actually.

I couldn't resist peeking out. A young man was rushing down the hall. He had a motorcycle helmet tucked under one arm, and the scent of wood smoke clung to him.

Joe . . . My mouth started to form the name, to call out to him.

I stopped myself just in time. The guy had just turned his head.

It wasn't Joe. I'd never seen him before.

Another man appeared, hurrying toward Motorcycle Guy. This one I recognized. It was Scar Guy. A pretty girl with dark, curly hair was right behind him. I recognized her, too. Chloe.

Motorcycle Guy was talking in a loud, excited voice. I tried to tune in, to figure out what he was saying.

". . . so I think we're good," he exclaimed to the others. "And now that I've taken out the other one, maybe the cops won't search so hard for the one we've got."

Chloe gasped. "You mean you killed him?" she cried. She sounded upset.

"Good work. Let's go tell the Big Boss," Scar Guy said, not sounding upset at all. "He's probably still in Kyle's room."

They all hurried away. The wood smoke smell faded. Alice tugged on my arm.

"Keep going," she whispered. "We're almost there!"

I tried to shake off the fuzziness. I was pretty sure I'd just heard something important. Who were they talking about? Who'd been killed?

"Hurry!" Alice called softly.

I realized I was standing still in the middle of the hall. Putting my legs into motion, I hurried after her. It was getting harder to keep track of everything. Maybe I just needed to focus on this one thing.

Following Alice. Getting away.

I could figure out the rest later.

She pushed open another door. This one was different from the rest. Heavier. But I didn't have much time to think about that before it was closing behind us with a clang. The sound echoed loudly. Or was that just because everything sounded weird to me at the moment?

We were in a dimly lit space. Stone walls stretched ahead, the passage narrow and cold. Ahead lay only solid darkness.

"The tunnels," I mumbled, remembering what Alice had said.

She didn't respond. Reaching into her pocket, she pulled out a small flashlight that looked like a kid's toy. Then she plunged ahead into the darkness. I followed, not wanting to lose sight of the tiny light. If the darkness swallowed me up, I might not escape it this time. . . .

After that there was a lot of walking. And more walking. And then even more.

I stopped trying to think. It took all my focus just to walk. To put one foot in front of the other and follow the little girl through the twisting, turning tunnels. What was that little girl's name again?

"Alice," I blurted out with relief after expending some effort in retrieving the answer.

She glanced back. "What?" she asked. "Hurry. Are you coming?"

"Coming," I mumbled. The little girl was Alice. She was one of the Misty Falls Lost. Only she wasn't lost anymore. Was she?

Things went on like that for a while. One minute I wouldn't be sure who or where I was. Then everything would come back to me in a rush. Then it would be gone again.

It was the weirdest feeling I'd ever had in my life.

More time passed. How much? I had no idea. Maybe hours. All I knew was that I was exhausted. I could barely keep up with the little girl.

But Alice never seemed to run out of energy. She led the way, stopping at every fork in the tunnel. Every intersection. She would peer at the walls, then start walking again.

I looked at the walls too. There were marks on some of them. Odd little jumbles of blobs and circles and lines. They made no sense to me at all.

Walking, walking, walking. The tunnels were full of muffled sounds. Echoes and clangs. A few times I thought I heard footsteps behind us.

"Did you hear that?" I asked one of those times, stopping short.

Alice glanced back. "Hurry!" she called. "I think we're almost there."

She rushed on ahead, and I followed. Mostly because I couldn't figure out anything else to do.

Finally we reached a dead end. Solid stone walls rose all around us.

"Now what?" I asked, struggling to remember what we were trying to do.

Oh, yeah. Escape.

Alice was shining her little flashlight all around, looking frantic. "There should be a way out!" she cried, sounding ready to burst into tears. "There has to be a way out! I know this is the right way, Justin taught me the marks!"

She scurried off back down the tunnel. I saw her little light pause near the last intersection a dozen yards back.

Meanwhile I looked around. Some of my ATAC senses were drifting back at last. This was supposed to be an escape route. The way Justin had gotten out. So where was the door?

I tapped on the walls. Solid stone. And there were no marks here.

Hang on. How could I see that? Alice and her flashlight were too far away.

I looked up. The ceiling was low here, just a foot above my head. Dim light showed up there, a thin line of it, forming a big square.

A hatch!

My mind cleared a little more. This was it! It had to be. The escape route. A hatch rimmed by moonlight.

I reached up and felt wood. Taking a deep breath, I gave it a shove.

CLICK!

Cool, fresh air rushed in as the hatch cracked open above me.

Burning Questions

The flames danced around me, higher and higher. Every tree in the forest seemed to be on fire. I spun around, coughing as smoke surrounded me. There was no way out!

Then I spotted it. A tiny opening in the wall of flames. Maybe an animal trail that had beaten down the grasses. Or a rocky streambed. Whatever. I didn't wait to ponder it. I just dove forward, closing my eyes and holding up my arms to protect my face.

Searing heat. Deafening crackling all around me.

Then—cooler air. A breeze on my hot face. I was out the other side!

I dropped and rolled, quickly smothering the

tiny fingers of flame that had tagged along and were licking at my clothes. Then I stood up, gulping in the relatively fresh air.

But the fire was still spreading. I had to get away before it caught up to me again.

I ran down a rocky hillside, coughing on the smoke that seemed to be drifting everywhere. It was hard to see or hear much.

But then I heard it. A welcome gurgling sound.

I followed it, fighting my way through the smoke. There it was—a broad, shallow, tumbling stream!

Splashing in, I hardly felt the cold as the water soaked me to the skin through my singed shoes and pants. I waded downstream a few yards before making my way to the opposite shore.

When I climbed out, I looked back. The fire was still hungrily devouring everything in its path. But I was pretty sure it wouldn't be able to jump the stream.

Whew!

Then I realized I wasn't out of the woods yet. Literally. I was still lost in the wilderness. Wet, hungry, and cold. In the middle of the night. With no idea where I was or how to get back.

At least there was a moon. Noticing a mountain rising out of the scrubby trees up ahead, I took a step toward it. Maybe if I climbed up there I'd be able to see something when morning came. . . .

"Ow!" I yelped as I felt my toe catch on something.

Looking down, I saw that I'd stumbled over a large rock. No, a *pile* of rocks.

I blinked at it.

"Hey!" I blurted out in surprise.

Then I fished out my flashlight. Luckily, ATAC makes sure our gear is all waterproof. And I guess heatproof, too. The flashlight had only melted a little bit around the edges, and it still worked when I hit the switch.

I aimed it at the rock pile. Yep—just as I'd thought. It wasn't something that could have happened naturally. Not unless the local bears and rabbits were into decorating.

In fact, this looked like one of those little cairns I'd noticed in the woods near our campsite. A *lot* like it!

For a second I was excited, thinking that maybe I was close to our campsite after all. Then I shook my head, realizing that was stupid. I'd traveled on that bike for more than half an hour. And I have a decent sense of direction. I was pretty sure we hadn't doubled back.

Okay, call me crazy. I knew I should be focused on my own survival and nothing else. But I was curious about the stone piles. What did they mean? Could they have anything to do with the mission?

Besides that, Bailey had thought the piles might be trail markers. If she was right, could this little stack of stones lead me out of here?

I shone my flashlight around as I thought about it. The beam landed on something else.

A footprint.

It had been left in the mud at the stream's edge. By a boot several sizes larger than my own. The print was about two feet from the little pile of stones. Pointing away from it.

I glanced from the print to the stone pile and back again. Something finally clicked in my mind.

"That's it!" I blurted out. "It *is* a directional marker!"

The stones seemed like a random pile. But when you looked closer, the smaller ones were all clustered on one side of the larger base stone.

As if pointing off in that direction!

I couldn't believe I hadn't seen it before. Then again, I'd always left that kind of thing to Frank. He was the one who liked those sorts of puzzles and brain teasers. Maybe his nerdiness had rubbed off on me more than I'd thought.

The fire was still raging away on the far side of the stream. I glanced back at it, feeling a twinge of guilt. Wondering if my campfire had started it. It seemed almost impossible. For one thing, I'd taken all the usual precautions. Plus, my fire had been almost out when I woke up.

Then another thought occurred to me. Could that footprint have something to do with the fire? It looked pretty fresh. . . . Either way, I figured I'd have to worry about it later.

Right now I wanted to see where the cryptic trail marker was pointing. Maybe it really would show me the way back to civilization.

"Worth a shot," I murmured to myself. "It's not like I have any better plan right now."

So I walked in the direction the marker was pointing. The way the footstep was going.

Who did that footstep belong to? I turned over the possibilities as I trudged along, my wet shoes sloshing with each step.

Best-case scenario, it could have been left by a park ranger. Maybe a hiker. Someone heading back to the park entrance.

Then again, what if our mystery kidnapper had left it? What if he'd set that fire to try to take me out? I could be walking straight into danger.

Or straight to wherever they were holding Frank.

In any case, I figured it didn't hurt to be careful.

So I clicked off my flashlight and made my way along by the light of the moon.

Ten minutes later I wondered if that had been a mistake. I'd walked a long way with no other markers or other signs I was on the right trail. What if I'd missed something?

I was debating whether to turn back when I saw it. Another marker! "Yes!" I whispered.

This marker pointed off to the left. I headed that way. The trail led through some thick woods, so I had to use my light again.

When I emerged from beneath the trees, I saw another marker. It sent me angling off in another direction.

After that, it was just a matter of keeping my eyes peeled. The markers appeared whenever I was supposed to shift direction. By now I was at the foot of that small mountain I'd seen earlier. The going was pretty rough, and I was relieved when I found a marker pointing me across a broad, grassy meadow.

I started across it. The going was a lot easier here.

But there was nowhere to hide, a realization that hit me hard when I heard a weird, metallic clanging sound somewhere very close by.

I hit the ground, hoping the tall meadow grasses would hide me. Then I looked toward the sound.

My heart pounded. I carefully reached for my

flashlight. It wasn't much of a weapon, but it was all I had.

If I was about to meet the Misty Falls kidnapper, I wasn't going down without a fight.

"Ugh!" someone grunted.

I lifted my head carefully, trying to get a look. Just in time to see something rise out of the ground. It looked like a wooden door or hatch.

Huh? What was a hatch doing out here in the middle of nowhere?

I was still trying to figure that out when someone hoisted himself out of the hatch, collapsing onto the ground outside. Then he used the open hatch door to climb to his feet. That's when I finally got a good look at him.

"Frank!" I shouted.

Yeah, I know. I hardly believed it myself. But that was my brother who'd just climbed out of a hole in the ground right in front of me!

Leaping to my feet, I raced over to him. He let out a cry of surprise and jumped back.

SLAM!

The hatch door fell shut.

"Dude!" I cried as I reached him. "I can't believe it's really you! Where were you?"

Frank hardly seemed to notice I was there. He fell to his knees and scrabbled at the hatch.

"Oh no!" he exclaimed, his voice sounding hoarse and kind of wobbly. "Alice? *Alice!*"

I wasn't sure what was going on. But I could tell he wanted to get that hatch open again. So I crouched down and tried to help.

The hatch wouldn't budge.

"It must've latched from the inside when it fell shut," I said.

Frank bent over the hatch. "Alice!" he yelled. "You have to unlatch it!"

"They're coming!"

My eyes widened. A tiny, scared voice had just cried out from beneath that hatch!

"Who's that?" I asked. Frank looked frantic. "Reach up as far as you can!" he shouted. "Reach up and undo the latch, Alice! Hurry!"

The next thing we heard from below was a muffled scream. Then some shuffling and thumping, like the sounds of a brief struggle.

Then silence.

"Oh no!" Frank cried out. "They were following us after all. They caught up to us and captured her!"

"Huh? Who?" I was still majorly confused. "Where were you? What's down there? What's going on?"

Frank turned to stare at me. "I have no idea."

ound

"I finally got a signal." Joe shimmied down the trunk of a massive pine. "Rich is sending out a rescue party right now. Good thing ATAC embeds a GPS tracker on our cell phones, huh? Otherwise who knows how long it'd take them to find us."

I nodded. Joe had climbed the tree, figuring getting up high might help his phone pick up some reception. Luckily, it had worked.

"At least now we'll be able to get some answers," I said, glancing over at the hatch. "The cops should be able to break through into the tunnels. Then all they have to do is find their way back to the compound."

Joe shook his head. "I still can't believe all those missing kids are down there somewhere."

I was having a little trouble believing it all myself. My head still felt as if it was stuffed with cotton candy, which didn't help.

But in a way, that helped me realize just how true it was. The compound. The weird memory-fogging drugs. The missing kids, alive and seemingly well.

Alice.

"I hope they don't punish her too much before we get there," I said, wincing as I remembered that final, muffled scream. "She just wanted to find her brother."

"I just hope they don't all scatter before we get there," Joe said. "You know. Pack up everything and disappear to some other location."

"It would be tough to pack it all up," I said, thinking of everything I'd seen down there. "Even if the people are gone, I'm sure there will be plenty of evidence to help us track them down."

"Hope so. It's about time we got this mission wrapped up." Joe put away his phone and sat down with his back against the tree trunk. "At least it sounds like we'll have a happy ending this time, right? You said you saw most of the missing kids down there."

"Well, a few of them, anyway." I paused, letting my sluggish mind run through the events of the past two days. Thanks to Joe, I now knew that was how long I'd been down there. "There was Alice, of course. And Kerry, the second kid who disappeared. She's almost all grown up now. I'm pretty sure I saw Kyle, and I think Luke was down there too. I saw a few others who probably fill out the list."

"And Justin, of course." Joe sighed. "I still don't get it. What are they doing with those kids down there?"

"You got me. They don't seem to be mistreated."

"Other than being snatched away from their parents and forced to live in some underground bunker, you mean?"

"Yeah." I grimaced. "Other than that."

Joe stood up and started pacing. "I guess we'll find out soon enough," he said. "All we need is to get into that place, and we'll figure it out."

I yawned. "Agreed. Look, it's been a long night. Can you keep watch and wake me when the cops get here?"

Joe shook me awake. "Posse's here, bro," he said.

I sat up, blinking. Judging by the position of the moon, I'd slept for at least an hour. Maybe longer.

I was still tired, and I had a raging headache. But my mind felt a lot clearer than it had before.

Lights and voices came from farther down the slope, along with the roar of motors. The rescue party had come in on ATVs.

"Up here!" Joe shouted, waving his arms.

I joined in. The rescuers heard us and roared toward us. Rich Cole was in the lead, his trademark cowboy hat perched on his head. I'd never been so happy to see a cowboy hat in my life. Five or six other cops were right behind him.

There were a few minutes of confusion. Basically, Rich and the others just kept staring at me and saying, "I can't believe it!" over and over again.

I knew how they felt.

Anyway, eventually Joe and I got our stories told. When he heard about the hatch, Rich strode over to take a look.

"Door's made of wood," he said. "Somebody grab an ax and let's see if we can get to the bottom of things."

An officer I didn't know hurried back to the ATVs. A minute later he returned, hoisting an ax. He started attacking the hatch door with it.

The rest of us moved back to avoid the flying chunks of wood. "Hard to believe," Rich said. "All those kids—still alive and well after all this time."

"Guess the bears weren't to blame after all," another cop commented.

"Yeah," Joe agreed. "And I'm really looking forward to finding out who *is* to blame."

"Me too." Rich glanced at me. "You say you didn't get a look at this boss fellow?"

"Not really." I thought back to that scene with the screaming little boy. Kyle. The memory was dim and faded around the edges, like a barely remembered dream. But I was pretty sure the man everyone called the Boss had been there. "It was a man, I saw that much. Average height, dark hair. That's all I got."

"Hmm," Rich said. "Well, I guess we—"

KA-BOOOOOOOM!

The hatch exploded in a burst of noise and flame. The cop with the ax was tossed aside like a rag doll. The rest of us jumped back, raising our hands to shield our faces from the rocks and dirt shooting toward us like missiles.

"What was that?" Rich shouted. "Nate! You okay?"

There was an ominous rumble, and the ground started to shift and roll beneath us. Half the valley seemed to be collapsing under our feet!

"Run!" someone shouted. I think it was Joe. But I didn't stop to check. I was too busy running.

When the dust cleared, everyone was okay. Well, the cop with the ax was looking a little dazed, and one of his arms was bent in a whole new direction. One of the other guys had twisted an ankle. Aside from some cuts and scrapes, that was all.

But even with my mind still not quite back to full capacity, I knew what this meant.

The tunnel was gone. Caved in by that explosion. One look at the new landscape of the valley was enough to tell me that beyond a shadow of a doubt.

We had no way of finding our way back to that compound.

"Never mind, bro," Joe said. "We'll find it. How far away could it be?"

"Far," I replied bleakly. "I'm not sure exactly how long Alice and I walked. But I'm guessing that place has to be miles from here. I don't even know what direction we were going."

Joe didn't answer. He just stared at me. I knew what he was thinking, because I was thinking the same thing.

Now what?

FRANKLIN W. DIXON

THE HARDY BOYS

Undercover Brothers®

INVESTIGATE THESE TWO ADVENTUROUS MYSTERY TRILOGIES WITH AGENTS FRANK AND JOE HARDY!

#28 Galaxy X

#29 X-plosion

#31 Killer Mission

#32 Private Killer

#30 The X-Factor

#33 Killer Connections

From Aladdin
Published by Simon & Schuster

31901047529229